# ARCADY'S
# G●AL

# ARCADY'S GOAL

WRITTEN AND ILLUSTRATED BY

## EUGENE YELCHIN

HENRY HOLT AND COMPANY

NEW YORK

Henry Holt and Company, LLC

*Publishers since 1866*

175 Fifth Avenue

New York, New York 10010

mackids.com

Library of Congress Cataloging-in-Publication Data

Yelchin, Eugene, author, illustrator.

Arcady's goal / written and illustrated by Eugene Yelchin.

pages    cm

Summary: When twelve-year-old Arcady is sent to a children's home
after his parents are declared enemies of the state in Soviet Russia, soccer
becomes a way to secure extra rations, respect, and protection but it may also
be his way out if he can believe in and love another person—and himself.

ISBN 978-0-8050-9844-0 (hardback) — ISBN 978-1-62779-291-2 (e-book)

1. Soviet Union—History—1925–1953—Juvenile fiction. [1. Soviet Union—
History—1925–1953—Fiction. 2. Soccer—Fiction. 3. Communism—Fiction.
4. Foster home care—Fiction.] I. Title.

PZ7.Y3766Arc 2014    [Fic]—dc23    2014016088

Henry Holt books may be purchased for business or promotional use.
For information on bulk purchases, please contact Macmillan Corporate and Premium
Sales Department at (800) 221-7945 x5442 or by e-mail at specialmarkets@macmillan.com.

First edition—2014

Printed in China by South China Printing Co. Ltd., Dongguan City, Guangdong Province

1  3  5  7  9  10  8  6  4  2

Fewer than a dozen photographs of my family survived
the turbulent history of the Soviet Union, the country of
my birth. The photograph above inspired this book, and it
is the one that I most treasure: the Red Army Soccer Club
in 1945. The captain of the team is in the middle row, third
from the right. He is Arcady Yelchin, my father.

**I'M A RISK TAKER.** That's why I score like crazy. I score on the go, with the ball in the air, with my back to the goal. I score in all weather. Dirt, mud, or ice, I score. Today it's pelting rain. The ball is heavy, caked with mud. I beat Dimka on the dribble and push the ball through the puddles. He splashes after me, grabbing at my coat. Grabbing is against the rules in soccer, but here no one plays by the rules.

We play in a yard with a fence on all sides, the stakes of the fence are sharpened to knifepoints.

The barbed wire above the stakes keeps us from climbing. Penned in like that, every kick has rebound potential. Half the goals I score on the rebound, me passing to myself. Who else would I pass to? Our soccer is strictly one on one. The guards won't let us team up.

Huffing and puffing, Dimka is knocking himself out to keep me from scoring into his goal. It's not really a goal, it's just an old potato crate on its side. Potato crates are easy to find, but not the potatoes.

I'm about to kick the ball in when Dimka grabs me by the coat and spins me around. *Whoosh.* The fence flickers by. I lose sight of his goal, but that doesn't stop me. I back-heel the ball through his legs. The ball slams into the crate, planks shooting out in splinters.

Goal!

My pals are watching the game from under the sagging tarp. No one cheers. Why would they? I've beaten every one of them by now.

Dimka reaches deep inside his wet sweater, digs around awhile then pulls out a package wrapped in soggy newspaper.

"Here," he wheezes. "Pig out, champion."

He hands the package over, but when I try to take it, he doesn't let go. Our hands are in a tug of war. I look up to see his eyes shiny from hunger. He can't hold my stare and lets the thing go.

He slogs away while I unwrap the package. An eighth of bread, our daily ration.

Under the tarp, my pals rise up to watch me eat my bread. I feel sorry for them, but what can I do? It's not my fault I'm that good at soccer.

"Hey, Dimka!"

He turns just in time to catch the bread I toss.

"Keep it," I say. "I'll win it next time."

**JUST THEN** someone hollers into my ear, "Got you, criminal!"

It's Butterball, our wisecracking director. A guard is by his side, one of the rougher ones. Butterball never shows up in the yard without a guard, sometimes two. The guard grabs me.

"Setting up illegal soccer games, Arcady?" Butterball bellows. "Cheating poor orphans out of their bread rations?"

"Get lost."

"Hold your tongue, boy! Ready to go back to solitary? No kicking the ball there."

The guard gives my arm a squeeze. Right then, I spot the ball flying our way. Dimka must have kicked it. I duck and the ball thuds against the guard's overcoat, smearing it with mud. My pals take off shrieking from under the tarp, splashing through the puddles. The guard cusses, lets go the scruff of my neck, and charges at them, shouting "Disperse!" and "No assembling in groups!"

The moment the guard lets me go, I make a move, but Butterball is ready for it. He is fat but able.

"Not too fast," he says, reeling me in.

"What do you want?"

He glances over his shoulder then looks back at me and squints his itty-bitty eyes. "Not much. Just show off your soccer skills for some important people tomorrow."

He's a sly one, that director, you can't trust him. He wants me to show off my soccer skills, but it was he who outlawed soccer when someone snitched we were playing for food rations. Strictly forbidden, he said, but it's his fault there's never enough food to fill our bellies. We have to pull through somehow.

"The government inspectors are here tomorrow to check on us. Any small thing that's not to their liking, heads will roll," Butterball whispers, leaning in close. "I know for a fact, the inspectors are all soccer fans. We show you beating one kid after the next, they'll forget all about their inspecting." His itty-bitty eyes dart around. "Just in case, Arcady, I'll line up some mama's boys against you."

Butterball is waiting for me to agree. Let him wait.

He leans in even closer, brushing his clammy nose against my forehead. "I heard of cases," he whispers, "where some inspectors only pretend to be inspectors. They are soccer coaches searching children's homes for new talent. Soccer is big, son. The important thing is to be in the right place at the right time." He shuts one eye and fixes me with the other, this must be a wink. "Trust me, Arcady, you are in the right place."

Butterball would say anything. He's a liar. But catch him telling a lie, what does he care? I've never seen him blush once. I know for definite that if a soccer coach sees me score, nothing will happen. Butterball told us a million times that children like us are not allowed to be team players.

While he keeps on blabbering, I stare at his mouth moving but can't hear a thing. From his mouth a delicious smell flows into my nostrils. Sausage, fried onions, and something else I don't have a name for, goose liver maybe. I go numb from smelling such foods.

Everyone knows Butterball is stealing our food. Take a look at his gut and smell his goose-liver breath. But the truth is, he needs more food than most. Besides us, he has to feed nine in his family, and one still in diapers. Everyone has to get by somehow, but it's harder for him. Tomorrow the inspectors might get wise to his stealing and ship him off to hard labor or worse. Who'd feed his little kids then?

"I'll do it on one condition," I say.

"What is it?"

"Two bread rations for each game I play," I say. "One for me and one for the loser."

Butterball's bald head shines in the rain, a raindrop hangs off the tip of his nose. He grins. "You got yourself a deal, son."

**3**

**IT'S STILL DARK** when the guards drive us out
of our bunks and out of the dorm. Shouting and

blowing their whistles, they hustle us down the stairs. At the bottom landing, there are more guards with dogs barking and snapping at us as we pass. These dogs are as mean as the guards, but not as dumb.

In the yard, Butterball bellows through a bull-horn, "Fall in, criminals! Fall in! Form lines!" Then he gets mad at the guard. "Put the runts in the front, blockhead!"

Looking for places, we push and shove each other. It's a mess, but the guards straighten us out in no time. Smack first, talk later, that's our guards.

"Children of the enemies of the people!" Butterball booms through the bullhorn. "Do not forget what our humane government has done for you. The government has put a roof over your heads, has given you food, shoes, and medicine. It has given you free education. But what did your parents do? They were accused of crimes against our people. They were punished and left you orphans. Remember, children, you are better off without such parents. When the government inspectors visit us today, show your loyalty and gratitude. No wisecracks. No monkey business. Questions?"

None of us know what he's talking about. Ask what our parents have done, and each one of us would say our mom and dad were good.

**THE DOGS BARK** when a slick city car rolls into the yard. A loudspeaker fixed to a pole bursts into army march then cuts off. After some hiss and crackle, the march starts over. The car slows through the puddles to keep its polished sides free of mud and stops at the steps where Butterball stands at attention. The driver in police overcoat, fully armed, hops out and swings open the glossy doors. Inspectors in thick woolen coats, fur hats, and good leather shoes heave themselves out. They are laughing at something the driver has said. None of them look at us.

Butterball, beaming with pride, steps up to the car. As each inspector climbs out, Butterball kisses him on one cheek, then again on the other, and after looking into the inspector's eyes with his moist ones, a third time. They must feel disgusted to slobber on each other, but that slobbering makes their greeting official. They always do it.

I know a hundred percent that Butterball lied to me about soccer coaches pretending to be inspectors, but still I scope each one of them closely. Not that I've ever seen a soccer coach in real life, but if I see one I'll know it.

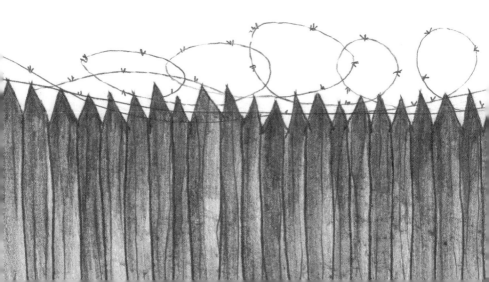

When the last inspector gets out of the car, Butterball leans in for a kiss. The inspector pulls back, frowning. He's not well fed or well dressed. Instead of a thick woolen coat he's got on a paper-thin slicker all crumpled and worn. He is hatless and to his chest he's clutching a beaten-up briefcase. He doesn't let Butterball slobber his face, but loops around him, steps into the puddle and stands there not minding it, staring at us with troubled eyes. He's no soccer coach for definite, but he's nothing like the rest of his pals either.

**BUTTERBALL SEATS** the inspectors in chairs under the tarp, treating them with hot tea and bagels. The loudspeaker belches out army marches. I play soccer. The inspectors cheer, clap, and call out strategic tips to me. Their tips are lousy, none of them knows a thing about soccer. I win game after game, earning bread for myself and for each kid that I beat, not that they know it. I kept my deal with Butterball a secret.

Instead of choosing mama's boys, Butterball lined up giants against me. On their last lap here, my opponents, some with mustaches, are closer to

grown-ups than to boys. They don't come near me as far as goal scoring, but they don't play to score. They play to stop me from scoring.

At every turn they slam me into the fence or push me into the mud. I suspect Butterball ordered them to make life harder on me, but I don't blame him. Knowing my skills, he aims to keep soccer interesting for the inspectors. Except that due to his instructions it's not soccer anymore. It's murder.

We keep to one rule: playing to the first goal. As soon as I score, I win.

The losing kid is out, I switch sides, and Butterball puts up another. After I beat six kids, I'm worn out, but Butterball puts up the seventh. His name is Akim, a big kid, our biggest. He's not one of my pals, he never even plays soccer. Not that he's playing it now, but he bangs into me and he kicks hard. Akim's line is bodily harm.

While the dumb kid is mauling me, I keep one eye on the hatless inspector, the one who refused to get slobbered. He's sitting with the others, but he's not drinking tea or chomping on bagels. He sits there frowning, looking around as if he's bothered by something. For no reason at all I want to bang in a real kicker for him to enjoy. Why I want to please him I'm not a hundred percent, but I pull all the stops, bent on beating Akim even if they have to carry me out.

The trouble with Akim, he takes plenty of room. Whatever I do I can't get past him. He's all knees and elbows. I bounce off him like a ball off the fence. I try again and again.

Like a wet bull, Akim sinks deep in the mud. I thud the ball between his legs, but he claps his knees together and the ball bounces back to me. I trap the ball with my chest, let it drop, and chip it over. The ball spins, flinging mud. Akim lifts his nose to look, and mud plasters his face. He cusses. When I loop around to grab the ball, he sticks his boot out and trips me. I fall. The inspectors clap and cheer, excited. Akim grins stupidly, looking at Butterball instead of the ball. The ball is stuck in the mud by the fence, a short stop from Akim's goal. If I get there first, I'll score. I fly up and run. Akim chases after me, but he's slow, I get there first. I thud the ball into the fence and spin around to follow it on the rebound. Just then, Akim head-butts me into the fence. The yard goes black. I feel myself sliding down and lean into the fence, gasping and watching

crazy spots and lights swirl before my eyes.

"Good game, boys!" hollers Butterball, his fat cheeks wobbling. "Tough as nails, this boy Arcady," he says to the inspectors, proud-like. "No feeling in him."

The loudspeaker hisses, crackles, and goes dead. In the sudden hush, the hatless inspector leaps up, knocking his chair sideways. "How could you be so cruel?" he says to Butterball in a shaky voice. "He's only a child!"

Butterball blinks his itty-bitty eyes. "What?" he says.

"Stop this game at once!" the inspector says and glances in my direction. Our eyes lock for a spell, and I nearly miss the next stupid thing Akim is about to do. He plunges into the puddle where the ball is twirling and, squashing it under his boot, turns to see if he can kick it into my goal from there. I dart after him, slide into a tackle and knock the ball from under his boot. The muddy ball lifts up like a heavy bird, knocks against the pole that holds the silent loudspeaker, and on a rebound whacks the hatless inspector square in the face. The loudspeaker hisses, crackles, and goes back to army marches.

**NOT A THING** has changed since the inspectors' visit. No heads have rolled. Not even mine for whacking the inspector. I'm owed six bread rations and six to the kids I beat, twelve in all, the seventh game we never did finish. I wait and wait for Butterball to give me the bread, but he is hushed on the subject. When I'm in his range of vision, the moron looks away. It's a good thing I kept the deal we made to myself, otherwise the kids would be counting on extra rations. But I aim to follow through. That goose-liver-breath owes me, if he forgot, he'll need reminding.

## CHAPTER SIX

One morning, I sneak away from the yard and climb the stairs to the door behind which Butterball sits on his rear all day. The guard leaps up from the chair next to the door. "Whoa, whoa," he cries. "Where do you think you're going?"

"To Butterball?"

"Don't call him that!"

He tries to smack me, but by then I'm kicking the door in. First thing I see is Butterball sitting behind the desk made of steel, his fat arms are up to the elbows in the open drawer, digging for something.

"Hand over the bread, Comrade Director," I say politely. "You owe me."

Butterball looks up, startled. His eyes dart to the window where a tall citizen is standing with his back to the door, looking out into the yard. Butterball screws his eyes at me and flashes a big grin.

"Look who's here, Ivan Ivanych! Our famous

soccer champion! We were just about to send for you, Arcady!"

The citizen turns from the window. It is that hatless inspector I whacked with the ball. He's got the same paper-thin, crumpled slicker on and he clutches the same worn briefcase. I'm not even surprised. I knew he'd be back to make me pay for that tackle kick.

I bolt back through the door, but the guard is there. He grabs hold of my ear. "I got him, boss!" he shouts to Butterball, dragging me by the ear back into the room. "We'll show you what's what, criminal!"

"Leave the boy alone!" the inspector cries and steps forward, raising his briefcase like a club.

The guard freezes and looks to Butterball, confused.

"Let go of the ear!" Butterball says.

The guard's mouth drops open. He blinks stupidly and lets go my ear.

"To the door!"

Soldier-like, the guard salutes Butterball and marches in reverse until his back slams the door shut. Then it's quiet.

I take in the situation. Not good. Only two ways out of this mess: the door and the window. The guard is blocking the door, and the inspector is standing in front of the window. I rub my ear, on fire from the guard twisting it, and keep my eyes peeled for either of them to make a sloppy move.

The inspector lowers his briefcase, sighs, and says, "Hello, Arcady."

Hello to you too, moron.

"Don't be rude, Arcady," Butterball says. "Say hello to Ivan Ivanych."

"It's all right," says the inspector. "He doesn't have to."

Something is fishy about this inspector. The way he beams in my direction you'd think he's glad to see me. He doesn't smile, but his eyes make me think of a smile. But don't believe it, the inspector is here for one reason only, to teach me a lesson. I don't care if they lock me in solitary, I'm not afraid of rats. But what if they ship me to one of those camps no one comes back from, or worse. Butterball said I'm finally old enough for the firing squad. They shoot you at twelve nowadays.

"Should we read the boy's file, Ivan Ivanych?" says Butterball. He lifts a thick brown binder out of the drawer, flips it open, and reads out loud, "Olenin, Arcady Alexandrovich. Born 1928 in Demkino, Moscow region. Father: Olenin Alexander Stepanovich. Mother: Olenina Elena Petrovna. Both arrested October 19, 1931. The charge: participation in a terrorist organization. Preparing to overthrow Soviet power and the defeat of the USSR in a future war."

"Enough, please," the inspector says sharply, but Butterball doesn't hear or maybe doesn't want to hear. He keeps on reading.

"Both sentenced to . . ."

"Enough!" The inspector pounces on Butterball and yanks the file out of his grabbers.

The opening to the window is as wide as a street. *Zoom!* I leap onto the windowsill, and just as I'm about to smash the glass with my boot, strong hands lift me off, set me down on the floor, and turn me around.

"Take it easy. You'll hurt yourself."

It's the inspector.

"Don't you remember me?" he says. "I watched you play soccer. You were . . . you were good."

He smiles!

His smile is too close, and I want to move away, but he's holding me, not roughly, gently. The binder he snatched from Butterball is under his arm. Not that I care, but the binder is open and I can't help seeing what's there. Stuck to the front page are pictures: a man's and a woman's, two pictures per face. In one picture, the face is looking at you, in the other

you're looking at the side of the face.

Next to them is another picture: it must be of me, still in diapers. My ears stick out just like the man's in the picture, my eyes are as big as the woman's.

I knock the binder out from under the inspector's arm, and it flies open in a swirl of loose pages. The inspector staggers backward and falls, conking his head against the steel desk. *Boom*. The guard grabs me from behind. I back-heel into his privates. He gasps and loosens his grip. I dart into the corner, swiping a chair on the go. With my back to the wall, I hold the chair at the ready. Come and get me, comrades!

Nobody moves. Silence.

*Tap.*

*Tap.*

*Tap.*

Outside the window, a little gray bird is tapping on the glass. Butterball turns to look, his chair creaks, and the bird takes off. Butterball turns back to me.

"Put the chair down, Olenin," he says.

"Make me."

Butterball heaves his gut from behind the desk and waddles up to a safe distance.

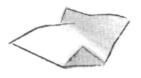

"Ivan Ivanych has come to adopt you, Arcady. You can go and live with him. It's allowed. Put the chair down."

I glance at the inspector. He's sitting on the floor, rubbing the back of his head. I keep the chair where I have it, and Butterball nods in approval.

"I know how you feel, boy. What reliable comrade would take in a child of enemies of the people?" He shoots a suspicious look at the inspector then turns back to me, smiling his biggest fake smile. "But I promise you this, Arcady. If you don't like it with Ivan Ivanych, you can come back home to us. You know we'll always treat you like a son."

The inspector looks up at Butterball, not just looks but really drills into him with his eyes. What happens next I've never seen before. Butterball's fat neck flushes red, then his ears, his nose, his whole bald head turns bright red. What a guy, that inspector! Just by looking he made Butterball hear his own stupid words.

**"LIGHTS OUT!"** the guard barks from the doorway and the dorm goes black.

"Moron," someone says in the dark.

"Who said that?"

A giggle.

"I'm warning you, criminals," the guard says in a tired voice. "No more fooling around."

He locks the door, bolts it, and shuffles away, coughing.

With the lights out, you can't see a thing in here. The glass in the windows is long gone, boarded up now to keep the cold away. The boards shut most of

the moon out, but not the weather. In the morning, the water in the washbasin is frozen. We sleep two or three to a bunk to keep warm. Dimka sleeps on my left and Turk's on my right. For a blanket, we pull a thin lumpy mattress up to our chins.

"You're not even related," Dimka whispers. "Who is he, anyway?"

"He's one of them inspectors," whispers Turk.

"What if he isn't? You should've checked his papers."

"If he asked me," Turk whispers, "I wouldn't go."

"Who's asking you?" whispers Dimka.

"But if he did."

Then they are quiet for a while.

"Something is phony about it," Turk whispers. "What's he getting out of it?"

"I agree," whispers Dimka. "Why would he stick his neck out for you?"

"He said I'm good at soccer."

"That's just plain stupid, Arcady."

"Why is that stupid?"

"You think he's adopting you because you're good at soccer?"

Someone cracks up in the dark above us. It's Leshka Surkov from the top bunk. He's not one of my pals.

"That guy's no inspector," he says. "He's a soccer coach for the Red Army Soccer Club, right, Arcady? He wants you to join in!"

Everyone laughs.

"Listen up, fellows, I'm serious," Leshka goes on. "Arcady is so good at soccer that after he joins the Red Army team, Fedor Brutko will beg him to take his center forward position!"

The guard bangs on the outside of the door. "Quit the racket, criminals, or lose your rations tomorrow! Last warning!"

Nobody pays the guard any mind. Everyone's too busy howling with laughter even though what

Leshka Surkov said is not even funny. The Red Army Soccer Club is our champion team, the best in the country. The captain is Fedor Brutko, number ten. Brutko is the Red Army's top scorer, the best soccer player alive. I should never have told Dimka that I pretend to be Fedor Brutko when I play in the yard. Dimka gave my secret away.

"Hey, Arcady," someone hollers. "Think you can score a goal for the Red Army?"

"You score a goal for them, pal, you'd be a big shot!" someone else shouts. "A soccer champion!"

"What if Arcady gets to be a soccer champion? Then what?"

"He'd be allowed things."

"Like what?"

"Like maybe they'd forgive him for what his mom and dad did!"

Of a sudden in the yard a dog begins to howl. The dog draws that howl out, raising it and lowering it, again and again, hanging on to it for a long while. Then just as suddenly as the howling started, it stops. When it does, no one laughs anymore. Dead silence. Maybe they're all sleeping, but I doubt it. They're too envious.

**THEY CLEARED** the yard in case some kid gets the dumb idea to dart after us, and now the guards stand around, watching the doorkeeper unlocking the gate. With all the chains, bolts, and padlocks to undo the doorkeeper takes forever. Ivan Ivanych and I are waiting. Inside his beaten-up briefcase are the adoption papers, signed and stamped. I'm out of here, it's official.

The kids cram the narrow space between the yard's fence and the brick wall. I can see their eyes through the cracks in the fence, watching. Nothing like this has ever happened here or in any other children's home I've been to. Ever since I was that baby in the picture in my file they've shipped me from one dump to another. I've been to a million of them, each one worse than the one before. But this one with Butterball takes the cake, for definite.

Looking up at the Butterball's window, I can just make him out behind the grimy glass. He's ogling us too, lifting something wrapped in butcher paper to his trap then lowering it then lifting it up again. Go ahead, stuff yourself, moron. I bet you're sorry for losing the best soccer player you ever had. What will you do now to please the inspectors? Lick their boots?

Ivan Ivanych blows his nose into a hanky, a big sound in the hush of the yard, and shoots a worried glance at the guards. Crushing the hanky into his slicker, he misses the pocket on the first go. I can see that his hand is shaking. A worried feeling comes off him so strong I feel it in my gut. I'm worried too,

but not as much. Whoever this Ivan Ivanych is, there's no telling, but one thing for definite, he can't be any worse than Butterball with his solitary or the guards with their dogs. I'm taking a risk on the guy, but he's taking a risk on me also. We are kicking the game off even, double zero.

The doorkeeper pushes aside the last bolt, rusted from rare use, and heaves the gate open. I glance over at my pals watching through the cracks in the fence. Bye, Dimka. Bye, Turk. Bye, the rest of you, losers. Will I ever see you again? At least I scored for you the bread that Butterball owed. He didn't want to give over the rations, but Ivan Ivanych backed me up.

I step over the metal strip of the threshold, and when I look up, I'm in the street. Out of nowhere, a bunch of birds shoots up into the clear sky, flapping their wings. A bright red tram clank-clanks along the shiny rails, and through the gleaming glass the faces of the passengers are good and kind. They smile in a

way that tells me the passengers know
Ivan Ivanych is taking me to his home,
and I can tell the passengers think that this
is good.

The tram rattles away, and a group of
tidy little boys run across the tracks, swinging their schoolbags and laughing.

"Alyosha!" someone calls. "Forgot your
lunch!"

One of the boys stops and looks across
the street where a nice woman is standing,
holding up a paper bundle. The boy darts
back across the tracks. He takes the bundle
from the woman, but when she kneels to hug
him, the boy wiggles out and runs back to join
the others. When the boy passes us, the smell of
freshly baked bread wafts from the bundle he is
stuffing into his schoolbag. He smiles at me, and
his smile tells me he knows everything too.

Everyone we pass on that street is happy for me. Even a policeman in a crisp new uniform, looking severely at me from the street corner, is clearly a good man, who is trying hard to hide his joy for me because he's on duty.

**I'VE ONLY SEEN** city streets and houses from the backs of the trucks hauling me from one children's home to the next, but now my feet carry me forward ahead of Ivan Ivanych as if they know the way. Now and then, I give him a quick look just to make sure he's there behind me. It's a big walk, we go different roads. There are houses with the windows open. Music from someplace, a woman is singing in a pretty voice. A cat is licking its paw. A potted plant. Behind a big glass window, all kinds of breads I've never seen before, sprinkled with salt, with sugar, twisted and rolled and studded with dark shiny things. I see myself in the glass, I see him, too, watching me. I move on.

Soon the streets are left behind and now there are trees and bushes. Under a huge sky, a dirt road cuts through a field. I breathe in deep, getting the smells. In the field, the cows are chewing on grass. We pass one real close. The cow looks at us with glassy eyes and flicks its tail. In the grass, a little stool stands crooked, and next to it, a pail full of milk. No one's around to guard it.

Ivan Ivanych's house is far, far away. The funny thing is, as we walk we don't say a word to each other. I am waiting for him to say something, but not a peep the whole way. Maybe he's shy, it happens to some people.

Finally we come to a shady street with fences on both sides. The fences are low, up to my chest. No barbed wire. Ivan Ivanych points to something, but it takes me a spell to spot what it is. It's a house set back away from the street, snuggled in what looks like an orchard. The orchard is full of trees and the trees are full of birds. The birds flap their wings and hop from branch to branch, chirping. There's no gate, no fence, just a beaten footpath that curves away from the street. We follow the footpath through the orchard. It loops around the trees, gets lost in the grass, shows up again, and at last bumps into the steps before the front door of the house. Ivan Ivanych walks up the steps, pulls at the handle, and the door opens. I pretend I'm not surprised he hadn't locked it.

"Welcome home, Arcady," he says and steps aside to give me room to enter.

Here I lose my nerve. I haven't been inside a regular home since I was in diapers. I don't even know what's in there. He waits patiently, holding the door for me.

*Chirp. Chirp.*

A bird lands on the top edge of the door, hops this way and that on stiff legs, jerking its tiny head.

Even from where I am
standing, I can see its
chest quiver. That's the
bird's heart beating. Birds'
hearts beat that fast, but
now my heart is beating even
faster. The bird pecks at something,
chirps, and shoots off.

Ivan Ivanych smiles, follows the
bird with his eyes, then looks back
at me, still smiling.

"Coming in, or what?"

**THE HOUSE SMELLS** so good inside my mouth fills up with spit. I swallow—he probably doesn't like people spitting on his floor—and look around. Clear glass windows, no boards, and in the bright sunlight, a table crammed with food. A jug filled with milk, a loaf of bread, and in a bowl, peeking from under a towel, boiled potatoes. All free for the taking, and he didn't even lock his door!

I don't want Ivan Ivanych to see me drooling, so I give the room the once-over, looking for other things of interest. There are doors in this room, more than one. Leading where? He sees me looking.

## CHAPTER TEN

"Need to go?" he says. "A toilet is behind that door."

I shake my head no, so he points to the other doors. "Behind this door is where I sleep, and behind that one is your bedroom."

"My what?"

"Your bedroom, Arcady. Take a look."

My bedroom? I never even had my own bed. I crack the door open and poke my nose inside.

"Go in, go in," he says. "It's yours."

The sunlight blasting through the open window makes me squint. And the noise! The chirping of the birds is louder in here than out in the orchard. The room is tiny, but he squeezed in a bed somehow, and what a bed: high, wide, and white, with something pink on top. I spit into my hands, rub my palms together and wipe them on my pants. Then with clean hands I lift the pink thing off.

A knitted square, weightless.

"My wife made it."

He stands in the doorway, smiling, but sadly.

"Your wife? Where is she?"

"She passed away, Arcady." He shrugs as if surprised that a thing like that could happen. "This was to be our baby's room, but Natasha passed away before she had a chance to have a baby."

He looks past me into the room at things I saw or didn't see or maybe didn't want to see: a rocking horse, a spinning top, a doll. I lift the fuzzy thing I'm holding.

"What's this?"

"A baby blanket."

"I'm not a baby."

"Of course you're not, Arcady." Ivan Ivanych blushes. "I don't know what I was thinking."

He steps up quickly to take away the blanket. I look at his hand, I look at the blanket, I hide it behind my back.

**"BEFORE WE EAT,"** he says, "we wash our hands."

"My hands are clean."

He looks. "I wouldn't call them clean."

He fills a bucket with water so clear you see right through it, and he soaps me up. Hands, face, neck, inside the ears even. I keep my mouth shut. He washes off the soapsuds and dries me with the softest cloth. He holds my hands in his, palms up, palms down, checking. He's got a pair of scissors at the ready. He says the scissors are for fingernails, but what's there to cut? I bit mine to the quick.

He frowns at my teeth. "Don't you brush?"

"Brush what?"

He takes a tiny brush, wets it, dips the bristles into a round box with something chalky, and rubs it against my teeth. The taste is so nasty I begin to gag. He hands me water in a glass and says, "Swish the water in your mouth, then spit it out." I nod and swallow the water. He sighs.

Better not scratch my head. He's liable to hunt for lice, but who can wait? I'm starving.

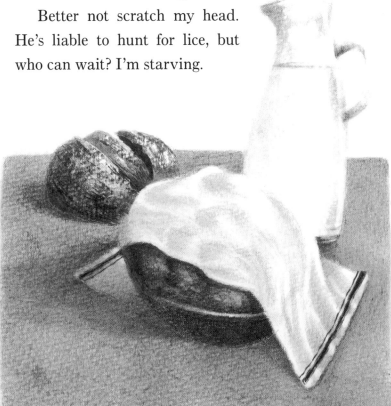

"Now you look like a regular boy." He grins. "Hungry?"

"No."

"Sit," he says. "You should eat something."

I sit where he tells me. He's banging some kitchen things in the corner. I can keep my eyes off his food, no problem, but I can't keep from smelling it. Those smells are something. It's a good thing I can be in control if I want to.

When Ivan Ivanych turns around, arms full of plates, forks, and glasses, his smile freezes. I'm cramming the whole loaf of bread in, ripping it apart with my teeth, wolfing it down in huge chunks. The bread is not as stiff as I'm used to. It is squishy, and it begins choking me. I snatch the milk jar. *Gulp. Gulp. Gulp.* The milk is delicious. Thick and slippery, the stuff runs over my chin, down my neck and inside my shirt. When the jar is empty, I slam it down a little too hard. The glass shatters. I swipe the pieces to the floor and pluck the towel off the potatoes. The biggest one, still warm, is turning red between my fingers. I must have cut my thumb on the broken glass, the blood is gushing.

The whole time, I'm on the lookout in case Ivan Ivanych decides to jump me, but he stays put, watching. After all his food is gone, I sweep the crumbs into the palm of my hand and open my mouth to toss them in, but he leaps at me and catches me by the wrist. "Can't you see glass in there?"

I open my hand to tiny diamonds twinkling in the thick of bread and potato crumbs and blood

from my thumb. He flips my hand over and shakes the crumbs and glass on the floor. I yank my hand away from him and get up.

"Let me see your thumb," he says.

I stick my thumb into my mouth to stop the blood and move away from him. On the windowsill there's some pretty red stuff inside a jar.

"What's in there?"

"In the jar? It's strawberry jam Natasha made . . . or what's left of it. Would you like some?"

Strawberry what? Never heard of it. I burp. "My favorite. Lay it on me."

"Lay it on you?" he repeats after me, maybe even a little sore. "Happy to, but first we need to tend to your cut and to the mess you made. This is your home, Arcady, not a pigpen."

**HE CLEANS MY CUT** with water, dabs some purple stuff on, and wraps my thumb with a see-through cloth. The cut doesn't even hurt, but I like him bothering with it.

"Let's take our chairs outside," he says, "and watch the sun go down."

Why he wants to do a thing like that I don't ask. Maybe that's what regular people do after a decent meal. I take my chair out and he takes out his. We sit side by side. The birds chirp, chirp, chirp. I watch them whir in and out of the branches.

On the way in, they carry bits of stuff, twigs maybe, shavings, blades of grass, but on the way out, their beaks are empty.

"What are they doing?"

"The birds?" he says. "You don't know?"

I shrug.

"They are making homes for their babies, Arcady. It's spring."

I never looked at a bird longer than it took to aim a rock at it. But now with my belly more than full I'm thinking what's the harm in birds? I bet it's good to be one. To know someone is making you a home.

"I want you to be happy here, Arcady," Ivan Ivanych says. "You will be starting school in the fall, but for now anything you want to do, you tell me."

"Like what?"

"You must enjoy doing something. What is it? Woodworking? Arts and crafts? Reading?"

"You said I'm good at soccer," I say, surprised. "That's why I'm here, right?"

"Because of soccer?" He shakes his head and makes a snortlike sound. *Snort, snort, snort.* Is that the way he laughs? Snorting?

"What's so funny?"

He quits snorting and tries to make a serious face, but his eyes are still laughing. "You must have a special dream about soccer?"

"What kind of a dream?"

"I don't know. Whatever dreams regular boys have. Probably playing on a champion soccer team? Am I right?"

I better keep my mouth shut. I told Dimka and look what happened. They all laughed at me. This one will be snorting.

"My dream is to play for the Red Army," I blurt out anyway.

"The what?"

## CHAPTER TWELVE

"The Red Army Soccer Club. The best team in the country."

"That's good, Arcady. If you work hard, one day your dream might come true."

"Why not now? All I need is a tryout."

"A tryout for the best team in the country?" He watches me for a spell to see if I'm serious. "What's the hurry, Arcady? Your whole life is ahead of you."

"What life?" I fire back at him. "I know what you're thinking!"

"What's that?" he says, pulling back a little.

"You think the Red Army won't take me, right? Because of what Butterball said?"

"Who's Butterball?"

"Never mind that!" I spring up, knocking the chair sideways. "Kids like me are not allowed to be team players, is that right?"

"Wait a minute, Arcady."

"You figure if you scrub my neck and brush my

teeth you can make me into a regular kid?" I'm yell-
ing now. "My mom and dad were enemies of the
people! That makes me into one too. You know
what it feels like to be the enemy? Do you? Do you?"

I feel water coming up to my eyes, so I turn away
quick, kick the chair out of the way, and run
back into the house and into the room
that was made for a nice little baby
but got me instead.

**"ARCADY?** Where are you?"

His shoes squeak into the bedroom, stop at the open window. He's looking out, figuring I broke loose, but then he turns away from the window and squeaks up to the bed. His knees hit the floor, his hands, and then his face, poking under the bed. He looks at me rolled into a ball in the dark. "Why not get into bed?"

Something is swelling in my belly, an awful feeling, like my belly is about to blow up. "I'm fine here."

He glances at the baby blanket against my cheek
but says nothing.

"What now?" I say. "Taking me back?"

"You want to go back to the children's home?"

"I don't care."

He grins. "You and Natasha would have liked
each other. She was a hothead like you."

He stretches out on the floor, too tall for this
small room. He jams himself between the bed and
the wall, legs bent, elbows spread, hands holding his
chin, eyes staring. "I married Natasha three years
ago," he says. "About this time, in the spring. We
moved into this house and right away she wanted us
to have a child. I wanted one too, but not right away.
Let's wait, I said. I didn't know yet that you couldn't
argue with Natasha, so I did, I argued. Not for long,
but it turned out to be long enough."

He stares right through me, seeing his wife instead of me most likely, then he blinks and sees me again. "She ran out of time to become a mom, Arcady, and I am to blame for waiting too long. It's all my fault." He looks again at the baby blanket I'm holding. "I'm aiming to bring you up as if Natasha and I were your mom and dad, do you understand? I owe it to her."

He tries to smile, but his smile doesn't work too well.

"I can't promise you the tryout with the Red Army Soccer Club, but if you want to play on a regular kids' team maybe I can help you."

"I'm not allowed to be a team player."

"What if I start a team of my own?"

I look him right in the eye, testing. "You're no inspector, are you?"

He shrugs. "Not like the rest of them."

"I knew it. You're a soccer coach."

He looks frightened for a moment, thinking, deciding about something. "I might be," he says. "If that is what you want."

As though he cares about what I want. I see right through him. He says he wants to bring me up as if he and his wife were my mom and dad, but what he really wants is to make his kids' team stronger. If not for my soccer skills, I wouldn't be eating strawberry jam in his house. Just as I think about strawberry jam, something gurgles and moves up in my belly.

"What's wrong, Arcady? Not feeling well?"

He reaches under the bed to touch my forehead. Something bursts inside my belly, and I puke all over his hand.

**IF ANY OF MY PALS** knew I sleep with a baby blanket, they would die laughing. Not that I care, I like my blanket. I snuggle with it under the covers and sleep until the birds wake me. Then I go out to watch them. Birds have it made, for definite. All they have to do is hop from branch to branch, chirp, and look for bugs to feed their babies. The babies are in the nests. It's hard to see the nests from below, but I know the babies are in there, always hungry. I can hear them screaming their heads off. I've been waiting for the babies to learn how to fly. That would be something to see. They'll fly wherever they please, who's to stop them? There are no solitary cells in the bird world, no Butterballs, no camps. They never even heard of enemies of the people. Of course, it would be enemies of the birds to them. But enemies of the birds would not be birds, most likely. Birds wouldn't do a thing like that to each other. Leave it to people.

**MY LIFE** with Ivan Ivanych? First class. We fight, yes, on occasion, but I let him win every time. He wants me to wash up in the morning? No problem. Brush my teeth, top and bottom? I do it. I don't spit on the floor. I don't cuss. All around I'm good. In return, three square meals a day with extra helpings. But he never gives me as much food as he did on the first day. I felt sick as a dog that day and the day after. That scared him. He wanted to take me to the hospital, but I flat out refused. I stayed in my new bed holding the baby blanket, getting better all on my own.

To cheer me up or maybe to remind me why I was there, he brought home a fat book with pictures. He calls it a soccer manual. On the cover an artist drew the Red Army's captain, Fedor Brutko, in lifelike colors. In the picture, Brutko is kicking the ball. The goal you don't see because the artist ran out of room, but you know it's a great kick. You can tell right away Brutko is about to score.

Ivan Ivanych showed me pictures in that book of soccer players passing the ball to each other along the dotted lines. He showed me what he called diagrams that I couldn't even begin to understand.

Team strategies. Tips from famous players. About a million words in that book.

"We can read this book together, Arcady."

I look away to show I'm not interested. "I know all that stuff, Coach."

"Coach?" he says, surprised. "Yes, of course. You can call me that if you want."

Ivan Ivanych is hurt that his book didn't grab me, but he pretends not to care. He takes to reading the soccer manual by himself. Every night he studies the book way past the lights-out time, marking pages in red pencil. He thinks I'm asleep, but I'm watching through the crack in the door. I like watching him.

**I'M OUT IN THE ORCHARD** waiting for the bird babies to fly when Ivan Ivanych shouts out the window, "Come in, Arcady, I've got something for you."

What else could he think of? I've got everything.

"What is it, Coach?"

"You'll see. It's a present."

He thinks he can throw me off, but I know what presents are, I heard kids bragging. Presents are things moms and dads give if it's your birthday or else a holiday. Today's not a holiday and when my birthday is nobody told me. Could be today. I quit bird watching and bounce into the house.

"The families didn't want to pay for the uniforms, but I convinced them," he says, all proud. "I said to myself, if Arcady wants to be a team player his team has got to look right."

On the table, neatly laid out for me to admire, are a shirt and a pair of shorts, stockings with two stripes at the top, shin guards, and boots. All brand-new and about my size. Plus a soccer ball made of yellow leather.

"What do you say, Arcady? Like it?"

I'm stuck in the doorway, halfway in, halfway out, undecided. I've never seen soccer gear in real life, only in his soccer manual's pictures. On the cover, Fedor Brutko is in red top to bottom.

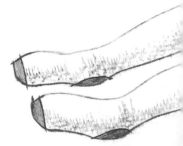

"Don't you want to try it?"

I shake my head no.

He's still smiling, like he thinks it's a joke. "What's wrong, Arcady?"

"The colors are wrong."

"What do you mean, wrong?"

"The colors should be red."

"Why red?"

"The Red Army team has red uniforms."

He quits smiling. "You are not joining the Red Army team, Arcady. You're joining a team of children."

He looks down at the shirt on the table, thinks about something then lifts it up to show me the number. "I had them put number ten on your shirt," he says. "Ten is only given to strikers, the most powerful forwards who score all the goals. I am making you a striker on my team, Arcady."

Here's my coach to you, loud and clear. All he

ever thinks about is how to make me score goals for him.

"What now, Arcady? You don't like your number?"

"I can't be ten," I say. "Ten is taken."

"Taken?" he says. "By whom?"

"Fedor Brutko."

"Who?"

"Brutko. The Red Army's captain."

I can tell he's getting sore, but he doesn't want me to know. "The Red Army's captain, Fedor Brutko, is number ten?" he says brightly. "Are you sure?"

I nod.

"Let's check," he says and looks around for his soccer manual. He finds it and stares at Fedor Brutko on the cover. "Red uniform," he says to himself, then to me, "You can't tell his number by this picture."

"He's ten."

He glances at me, annoyed. "They must say something about his number in the chapter on strikers." He wets his finger and uses it to leaf through the pages. "Here it is. Strikers." His eyes move quickly around the page then slower from side to side. "You're right, Brutko is ten." He holds up the book, open, for me. "You can read about him right here."

When will he stop shoving this book at me? I know I'm right.

He studies my face, then closes the book. "I should have guessed it before," he says and drops into the chair, looking dog-tired of a sudden. "They didn't teach you how to read."

**THE SHIRT** and the shorts are a little roomy, easy to breathe in, but the stockings are big. When I stretch the stockings over the shin guards, the heels stick out at the back of my boots. I roll the stockings twice at my knees so the stripes still show. I lace up the boots and wobble from the bed to the window and back. The bumps under the soles click-clack over the floorboards. Maybe running on them is faster. I fetch the ball and bounce it against the floor. The ball is tight as a drum. I don't feel like having Coach stare at me in his gear, so I slip out to the orchard through the window.

I look around for something to kick the ball into. I need a solid backstop. He doesn't have a fence or potato crates, nothing but trees. I could use the tree trunks, my aim is first class, but I don't want to trouble the birds. I dribble the ball around the house. The house is made of logs with windows cut on three sides, but the back wall stands solid. It's as good a backstop as any, better even than the rotten fence I was used to. I move away from the wall as far as the trees let me, roll the ball in the grass and hit it. The ball thuds against the wall and comes back. I don't let it touch the dirt and kick it back into the wall on the go. The boots are great and the ball is first class. I pound the ball with my right boot then with my left, whipping that wall so hard the house rattles.

"Arcady!" Coach shouts from the indoors. "Stop this minute!"

I slam the ball into the wall. *Bang!* Something falls inside.

"Arcady!"

The ball snaps back at me on the rebound and to spin it I crack it off center. The ball curves around the corner and drops out of sight. It's quiet for one tiny second, then, *bang*, glass shatters.

Next, Coach marches around the corner, the ball under his arm. "Look what you've done now," he says in a voice not loud but scary. "I told you to stop."

He stands over me, blocking the sky, his eyes are black dots. He's drilling into me with those dots the same way he drilled into Butterball in the children's home, as sore at me now as he was at Butterball. I wish he'd cuss at me or whack me, but he doesn't.

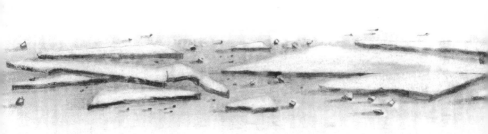

## CHAPTER SEVENTEEN

My throat makes a funny sound like maybe a hiccup. Water comes up to my eyes, but I don't let it out. He will never see me cry. Never.

He blinks and turns as if to walk away but doesn't. When he turns back, his face looks guilty. "Don't get upset, Arcady, it's not your fault. I gave you the ball." He looks at the ball in his hands. "Is it any good?"

"First class."

**COACH CLEARS OUT** what's left of the glass in the window frame, and I help by sweeping the floor clean. The broken pieces go into a pail that he takes outside.

"Now what?" I say when he returns with the pail emptied.

"Now we'll start learning letters." He sets the soccer ball on top of the table. "We'll make it related."

We sit down. He opens his briefcase, takes out a pencil, and makes a squiggle on a scrap of paper.

"Here we have a simple word, Arcady. Should we find out what this word is?"

CHAPTER EIGHTEEN

I nod, just in case. He smiles, pleased.

"Each word is made of sounds. Each sound is different, but if you join them together they make up a word."

I look past him at the broken window. He'd be madder if it was winter. Imagine if it was freezing outside and the snow was blasting through the hole. Butterball would have beaten the living daylights out of me. Not himself, he's too fat, he'd have the guards do it. I wonder how my pals are holding out. Still playing for food rations?

"Imagine, Arcady, that each sound is a soccer player. I know, I know, but try to imagine. What happens to soccer players when you join them together?"

"They make up a team?"

"Excellent, Arcady. They make up a team. The same with words. If sounds were soccer players then each word would be a team."

If I could get my pals to visit, we'd fix his

window in no time. We'd board it up. Rip a few boards from someone's fence, pull a couple of nails out, and we wouldn't even need a hammer. We could use that brick I saw behind the house. But what am I thinking? My pals can't visit. Butterball would never let them out.

"Are you listening, Arcady?"

He likes it when I nod while he's talking, so I nod.

"Listen to this word, I mean, to this team." He pushes his lips out and sounds off one bit at a time, "Bee . . . Aa . . . El . . . El." Then he does it again, and a third time. "Can you tell me what the first sound is, I mean the first player?"

"Bee?"

"Bee!" Coach says, excited. "You'll be reading in no time, Arcady."

Coach must have lots of kids on his team. Eleven at least, plus substitutes. Plenty of new pals to choose from. But what if they all turn out to be better at soccer than me? It's possible. What would he do then, send me back?

"Now listen carefully, Arcady. What is the word, I mean the team?" He makes the same sounds, but instead of drawing them out one at a time he says it faster, "Ba-a-a-a-l."

I look down at the ball he's holding then back up at him. He thinks I'm stupid.

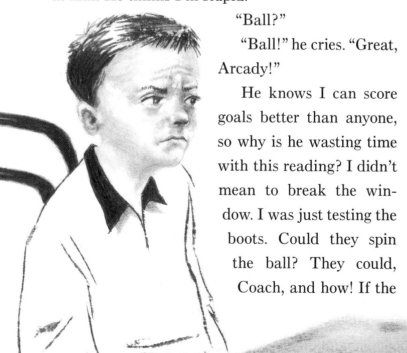

"Ball?"

"Ball!" he cries. "Great, Arcady!"

He knows I can score goals better than anyone, so why is he wasting time with this reading? I didn't mean to break the win- dow. I was just testing the boots. Could they spin the ball? They could, Coach, and how! If the back wall of your house were a goal with a goalie, we'd be one goal ahead by now.

"This is the easy part, Arcady. How many sounds, I mean, how many players are on this team? Bee . . . Aa . . . El . . . El? How many?"

"Four?"

"That's right, Arcady, four," Coach says with a big smile. "See, reading is not much different from soccer."

"No," I say. "It is different."

"How's that?"

"You can't have four. You have to have eleven."

"Eleven what?"

"Eleven players. In real soccer there are eleven players on a team. Plus substitutes."

He snorts. "Well, yes, Arcady, but some words are long and some are short."

"Then it's no soccer, Coach," I say, getting up.

He stops snorting. "Where are you going? We are not done yet."

"Listen, Coach, you took me in to score goals for you, right? What's reading got to do with it?"

Slam! That's his fist hitting the table. The ball bounces and shoots off somewhere. He's sore again.

"Sorry, Arcady," he says, not looking at me. "I'm not angry with you but with myself for that soccer team I suggested. The truth is . . ."

"That's what I'm talking about," I cut in. "We've wasted time. When will you take me to meet the team? I'm ready."

He looks up at me and heaves a big sigh. "Where did the ball go?"

I fetch the ball from behind the pail by the door and set it back on the table.

"Sit down," he says. "Show me some effort that you're willing to learn reading and I'll take you to meet the children. Is that clear?"

I nod.

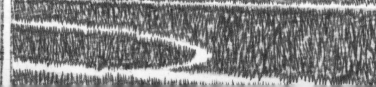

**THE SIZE** of the soccer turf knocks me out. I was best on a small patch of mud, but this thing is enormous. Imagine kicking the ball one on one on this spread? Forget it. You need eleven players to cover such ground. Eleven on one team, eleven on the other, and only one ball. What will I have to do to get it? Whatever it is, I'll do it and my new pals will back me up. That's what teammates are for, right?

I steal a sideways glance at Coach, standing next to me at the touchline. Today is my first drill with his team, but I'm not the only one worried. Coach looks white with worry.

"I know what you're thinking, Coach."

"What?"

"You're worried you made a mistake taking me on your team."

"I am?"

"For definite. But don't you worry. I'll score big for you on this turf. I promise."

He pats me on the shoulder. "I know you will, Arcady. I'm not worried about you." He looks up at a group of kids and grown-ups filing in through the soccer park's gate. "I have doubts about myself."

**THE KIDS LEAVE** the grown-ups behind and run to the benches. Most of the kids are about my size, some bigger. Their gear is the same color as mine, but the numbers are different. They're all talking at once, wanting to outshout each other. Everyone smiles. Why shouldn't they smile? By the look of these kids, none ever went without a home. What do they risk if they fail at scoring for Coach? Not a thing. But what if I fail to score?

My legs turn wobbly, so I sit on the grass. What a fool I was to leave the children's home. The bunks stunk and the food stunk and Butterball locked me up for any old thing, but I had nothing to lose in there. With Coach I left myself wide open. Anything could happen.

"Why are you sitting down?" Coach says. "Go meet the children."

He glances to where the dads group up, talking in low voices. "We'll start the practice directly, but first I need to speak to the fathers." He squares his shoulders, lifts his chin up, and marches off.

To get myself under control, I do the same thing Coach just did. I hop up, square my shoulders, lift my chin up, and march off to join my new pals.

With their heads close together they crowd the bench, laughing at a newspaper a chubby kid in the middle holds open in his lap. Not one looks at me when I get close except for a redhead with a million freckles who gives me a smile.

"Hello," Freckles says. "What's your number?"

I turn around to show him.

"Ten?" He whistles to show respect. "Ten is only given to strikers." He shakes his head as if he knows he doesn't have what it takes to be a striker. "Ivan Ivanych must think you're pretty special. What's your name?"

"Arcady."

"Arcady? You are the one he adopted?"

I shrug and look at the picture in the newspaper the kids are laughing at. It's a cartoon of a giant guard with a bayonet attached to his rifle stabbing some measly guy. On the guy's potbelly, right where the bayonet is poking through, the artist drew a cross all bent out of shape. Above the picture are a bunch of words. Coach has been drilling me for ages now, so I choose a short word and sound it out in my head letter by letter: E . . . N . . . E . . . M . . . Y. Enemy.

"What's so funny?" I say.

The chubby kid with the newspaper looks up at me. "Did you say something?"

"Maybe I did and maybe I didn't."

Chubby looks around at his pals as if asking, who is this guy? Meaning me. Now they are all staring.

"It's a cartoon," he says. "It's supposed to be funny. Want me to explain it to you?"

"I don't care."

He points to the giant guard. "See him? This is a border guard." He looks up at me with suspicion. "You know what those are?"

"I know guards."

"The border guards defend us from the German fascists," he says and sticks his finger into the crooked cross on the measly guy's potbelly. "This is the fascist's sign called a swastika. That's to let you know that when the fascists start a war against us"—he points to the measly guy—"he will be helping them."

"Why would he do that?"

"Were you locked up or something that you don't know anything?" Chubby says. "Because he is an enemy of the people."

I stare at him.

"Maybe he doesn't know who the enemies of the people are?" That's Freckles now. "He lived in a children's home." He smiles at me, trying to be helpful. "They didn't tell you there, right, Arcady?"

"Enemies of the people are spies and traitors hiding among us," Chubby explains. "My dad says we've been trying to get rid of them for years now, but they are like snakes with poison, no killing them all."

The kids begin talking all at once again, repeating what their dads said about enemies of the people and the coming of the war with the German fascists. I'm not interested in politics, so I walk away. Politics has nothing to do with me. I came here to play soccer.

**COACH DIVIDES US** into two groups, A and B. The groups line up, facing each other. I'm in group B, four kids to my right and four to my left. Coach, looking important with a whistle hanging around his neck and a ball under his arm, walks up and down between the lines, reeling off what he most likely learned from his soccer manual.

"As you know, children, a soccer team consists of ten field players and one goalkeeper. Eleven separate individuals. But what links these individuals together? What makes them a winning team that is greater than the sum of its parts? Anybody know the answer?" He looks at group A and then at group B. "Let me see some hands, children."

No hands go up.

"The answer is teamwork," Coach says. "Soccer is a team sport. Whoever heard of a game won by one player?"

The moment he says that he shoots me a worried glance. I bet he remembered me winning game after game by myself the day he showed up at the children's home. Seeing I'm not about to argue, he goes on.

"What is teamwork in soccer, children? Teamwork is passing the ball to each other, the most valuable skill to learn. Passing leads the team to success, but more important, passing lets us reward our teammates, relate to them in a positive way, and build long-lasting connections."

I look around at my teammates. The kids stare

up at Coach with their mouths open, eating up every word he says. What is he talking about? Reward and relate and long-lasting connections? Is he even talking about soccer?

Coach pulls a scrap of paper out of his pocket and stares at it for a while.

"Drill number one. Pass and support," he finally says. "Passing and receiving the ground balls. Everyone will have a turn." He looks at his paper again. "Prepare the ball with one touch, pass with the second touch. Keep the passing foot firm. Ready?"

He blows his whistle and rolls the ball to the first kid in group A. The kid tries to kick the ball but misses. Everyone laughs.

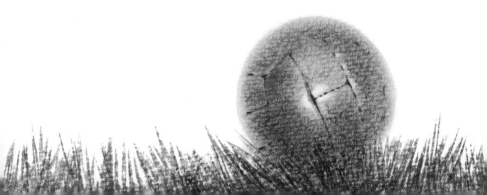

"Now, now, children," Coach says. "We are all learning here. Show a positive attitude." He blows his whistle again.

The first kid in group A kicks the ball to the first kid in group B then runs to the end of the line. The first kid in group B kicks the ball to the second kid in group A and runs to the end of his line. And so they begin messing up with the ball, kicking it any which way, half the time missing each other. Coach keeps blowing his whistle to  signal to each kid his turn to pass, and in between the whistling, he keeps saying, "Good, children, good. Don't forget to enjoy it."

Chubby, the kid who said that enemies of the people are like snakes with poison, stands across from me. After he receives the ball from a kid to my left, he tries to pass it to me, but misses the ball. The kids roll with laughter.

"Keep your eye on the ball, you idiot!" Someone hollers from the benches. One of the dads, a big guy with a red mug and bushy eyebrows, shakes his fist at Chubby. "Look sharp, son!"

Chubby's face turns red, and on the second try he manages to roll the ball in my general direction.

Coach gives me a smile. "Arcady's turn." He blows the whistle.

I let the ball roll up my right boot, lift it up, and let it drop onto my left boot. I juggle the ball from one boot to the other. I juggle it from thigh to thigh. I bounce it on top of my head. I bring it down, trap it with my chest, and lift it up again. I catch it with my shoulder. I roll the ball behind my neck to the other shoulder. I roll it back.

It's gone dead quiet on the turf. My teammates gape at me bug-eyed. Maybe they've never seen such ball control. In the children's home, the guards would lay odds on how long I'd keep the ball up, whacking me if I let it drop too soon. Now I can keep the ball up for ages.

"Pass the ball, Arcady," Coach says.

I juggle the ball in the reverse
order: around the neck
to the shoulder,
down the chest,
knee up to the top
of my head, up and
down, from thigh to
thigh, from boot to boot.

Coach blows his whistle.
"Arcady!" he says in a sharp
voice. "It is someone else's
turn. Pass the ball."

I roll the ball into
the grass, step on it and
look across at
Chubby. What
a mug, a young
Butterball, no
less. I'd love

to smack him
with the ball.
Square on the
forehead. Bang!
That would feel
fine. I glance at
Coach then back at
Chubby then down at the
ball. It gets so quiet you can hear someone's belly growl. When I lift my boot to kick
the ball, Chubby ducks, covering his face,
but I tap the ball gently to the little kid
next to him like I'm supposed to.
The ball bumps against his
boot, but the kid stands still,
afraid to touch the ball.
"I heard of him,"
someone says
at the end of

the line. "My uncle was on the inspection of the children's home in Kudelkino and he said a boy there was as good at soccer as anyone in the upper league."

"The children's home in Kudelkino?" another kid says. "That one is for . . ."

"That's the one. For the children of the enemies of the people."

Coach blows his whistle as if to stop the kid from talking, but it's too late. They all heard what the kid said.

"Let's not get distracted, children," Coach says. "Continue passing."

"I'm not passing to an enemy of the people," Chubby says and as if for backup looks over to the benches where his dad is watching us.

"Me neither," says the kid at the end of the line.

"That's right," someone else says. "None of us will."

Coach frowns. "Drill's over." He crosses quickly

between the rows of kids and plucks the ball off the grass. "Everyone can go home."

"Already?" Chubby says. "Can't we play a game without him?"

"No," Coach says, but just then some kid standing close snatches the ball from him and chucks it onto the turf. Everyone darts after the ball.

**WHAT THE KIDS DO** is the dumbest thing ever. It's not at all like real soccer. They run up and down in one big crowd trying to kick the ball at the same time. Now I know why Coach had me join. No one here knows how to score. But the dads don't seem to mind. They cheer and clap, rooting for their sons in loud voices.

"Go, Vanka, go!"

"Grab the ball, Petrucha!"

## CHAPTER TWENTY-TWO

"That's the way, Pasha, that's the way!"

Coach is not looking at me, but I know he sees me, waiting maybe for what I would do. Then it hits me, what am I standing around for? This is it. This is my moment. If I don't show Coach my scoring ability now, he'll ship me back to the children's home. It's that simple.

I charge onto the turf at full steam and take possession. This ball is mine, kids, I roar mentally at them, Stand back!

Some do and some don't. It's a mess, but I haul right into that mess. I beat four, five, six kids on the dribble, cut from the wing to the center, and hoof it straight to the goal. At about the penalty mark, they triple-team me. One kid is so eager he flings a shoulder at me. I ram into him. *Bam!* His rear is in the grass. The other two let me through, no questions asked. They know they can't stop me. It's in my eyes.

The goalie freezes when he sees me coming, his arms spread, eyes blinking, mouth open. Up close, I see who's scared stiff, my new pal, Chubby. You say enemies of the people are spies and traitors? You say they

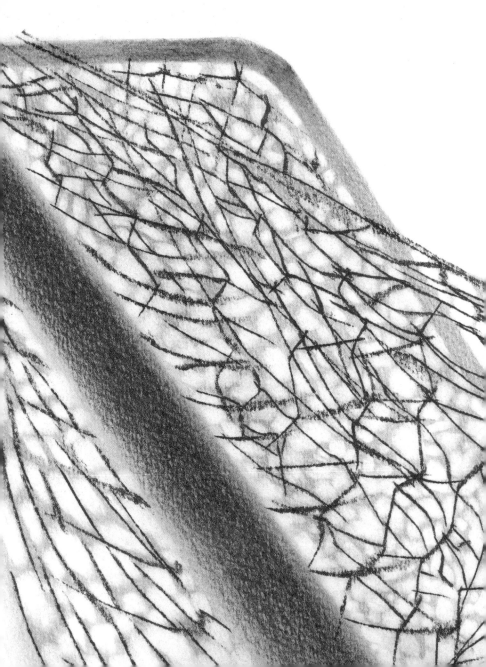

are like snakes with poison? You say no killing them all? Take this, little comrade, from an enemy of the people straight to you. A present. The cannonball slams into Chubby's chest. He squeals, and as if yanked from behind, he flies into the net. I wheel around to check if Coach saw it. How's this for a goal, Ivan Ivanych? Acceptable? But Coach is not even looking at me. He's looking at the fathers.

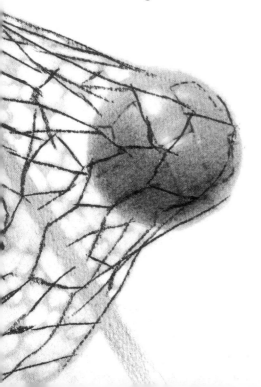

**"I'VE HAD IT,"** one kid says.

"I'm not playing," says another.

And they walk off. Just like that.

By the time I dig the ball out of the net, I'm the only one left on the turf. Over by the benches, the dads and the kids group up around Coach. I dribble the ball their way.

"Why didn't you tell us about the orphan?" I hear someone say when I cross the touchline. "I'd never have signed my boy up."

Coach shoots me a quick look. "There are no

orphans here, comrade," he says. "All our players have fathers."

I squeeze in between two dads to stand next to him. Both dads give me dirty looks.

"Is he even allowed to be a team player?" says one.

"Why wouldn't he be?" Coach says.

"Because of where you found him."

"It's not his fault what happened to his parents."

"Not for you to decide, comrade," says the other dad. "The authorities should be looking into this situation."

Coach's face turns white. "What situation?"

"We should have checked up on you first," another dad says.

"With all due respect, Ivan Ivanych, you fooled us," says someone standing behind me. "You're no soccer coach."

I look over my shoulder at the same red mug with bushy eyebrows that yelled at Chubby for missing the ball. Chubby stands next to his dad, sniffling.

"We all saw you peeking at your little papers," Bushy Eyebrows goes on. "Plain as day you never drilled a team before."

Ivan Ivanych opens his mouth to say something. Nothing comes out, but his mouth stays open. He blinks.

"You came to us claiming to be a soccer coach, Ivan Ivanych, and you gave us a big talk. You sold us on fancy uniforms. You said the kids would all be even on your team, but"—Bushy Eyebrows points his finger at me—"you gave your boy the best number."

The dads and their kids all wag their heads, some mumble rude things.

Ivan Ivanych clears his throat. "I can explain, comrades," he says in a whining voice not at all like his usual. "I wanted everyone to be even on our team to help Arcady grow into a regular boy. He deserves to be even with your children. If you want to discuss who gets what number, I'm not against it."

"Too late for discussions, Ivan Ivanych," Bushy Eyebrows says and looks away from him. "The uniforms are paid for, fellows. Those in favor of keeping the team raise your hand."

The dads shuffle and nudge one another, but no hands go up.

"Who's in favor of keeping the team but with a new coach, a real one?"

All hands shoot up.

"Ivan Ivanych?" Bushy Eybrows smirks. "You and your boy are out."

All at once, the dads and their kids begin to move about, talk in loud voices, and slap each other's backs. Ivan Ivanych staggers and grips my shoulder to steady himself. I shrug his hand off. He frowns at me, but I pretend not to care, busy staring at my boots.

"Look here, comrades," Ivan Ivanych calls out. "Listen to me a minute."

He has to say it again louder for the blank and surprised faces to turn, gaping as if they've never seen him before.

"I'm asking you not as a coach. I admit I'm not," Ivan Ivanych says. "I'm asking you as a father. Keep my boy on the team. Don't do it for him, but do it for your own boys. As fathers, your job is to teach kids to be kind to those not as lucky as them. Have a heart-to-heart with your boys. I know they will listen to you."

Bushy Eyebrows chuckles. "Ivan Ivanych is right, fellows. Let's talk to our boys. Mine could always use a good talking to." He screws his eyes at Chubby. "Next time, son . . ." He smacks the boy on the back of his head. "Look sharp for the enemy!"

Stunned, Chubby searches his dad's face, getting ready to bawl, but his dad moves his bushy eyebrows up and down, clownlike, and cracks up. Relieved, Chubby grins the stupidest grin. At that everyone laughs. The dads begin smacking their

kids and the kids begin to run around, shrieking.
"Look sharp for the enemy!" the dads holler, chasing after them as if they are playing some kind of
dumb game.

I steal a glance at Ivan Ivanych.

"What are you looking at?" he snaps. "Where's
my briefcase?"

"You are standing on it."

He snatches the briefcase off the ground.

"Coming or what?"

He walks off without waiting.

I start after him when someone calls,
"Ivan Ivanych? Wait a minute."

I turn around to see who's talking. It's
the only dad not running around like a
fool. Beside him, Freckles tugs on his
dad's sleeve and whispers into his ear.
The dad and his son look alike, both
redheads, one tall and one short.
Freckles sees me looking, and his

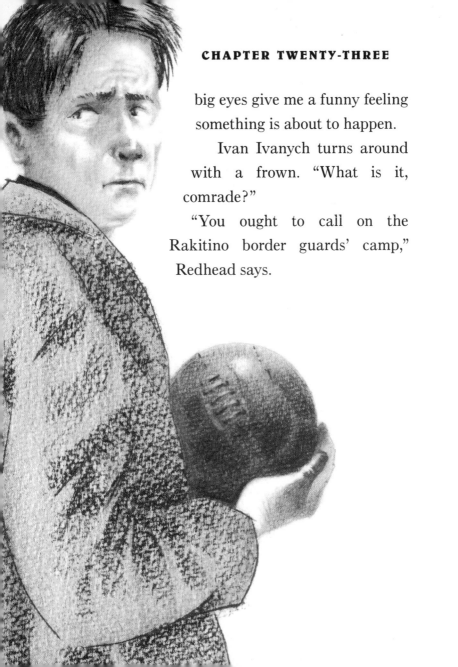

big eyes give me a funny feeling
something is about to happen.

Ivan Ivanych turns around
with a frown. "What is it,
comrade?"

"You ought to call on the
Rakitino border guards' camp,"
Redhead says.

Ivan Ivanych fixes his eyes on him with suspicion. "What for?"

"The soccer champions from Moscow are there. The Red Army Soccer Club. Training for the coming season."

Ivan Ivanych shoots me a glance then looks back at Redhead. "What of it?"

"They're trying out local boys to see if any are good for their youth team." Redhead looks at me. "They should take a look at your boy, Ivan Ivanych. He's a natural. Born for soccer."

Freckles smiles at me. His dad looks down at him, smiles also, and ruffles his kid's red hair. "My Grishka is not near as good as your boy but I'm taking him. I got the letter already."

"What letter?"

"A recommendation letter from the school district, what else? They won't let you near the camp without the letter. They are border guards, after all."

**WE ARE TAKING** a shortcut through the park. Ivan Ivanych is walking so fast, nearly running, I can barely keep up with him. Trees, statues, and flower beds flicker past.

"So what about it?" I say into his back.

"About what?" he says, without turning.

"You know. What that redhead said."

I cut in front of him and haul in reverse, face-to-face.

"You're taking me there, right? For a tryout?"

"After what just happened? Any one of them could still report us to the police."

"For what? A soccer tryout?"

"You don't understand, Arcady. We need to lie low."

"Why?"

"Never mind why! You've got more important things to worry about."

"Like what?"

"Like learning to read!"

"I know how to read."

"You call that reading?" He snorts. "How are you supposed to start school in the fall?"

Here he goes again with his school. As though school kids will treat me any differently from the kids on the soccer turf. But you wait till Fedor Brutko and his Red Army pals see me handling the ball. Then things will be different.

"Come back here this minute!" he yells after me. "Where do you think you're going?"

"To the Red Army," I yell back. "For a tryout."

I run across the grass, not looking back, not once, but when I'm far enough from him, I hide behind a tree and peek around to see what he does about me running. He's crazy mad. He lifts his briefcase above his head, then slams it into the dirt and kicks it. I take off running again. He sees me and charges after me. I am a quick runner, but he's working hard, hot on my tail, wheezing. I slow down to let him in close, wait till he tries to grab me then throw him a fake, leaning one way but turning the opposite. He stomps by and, failing to stop, runs full steam into a tree. *Bang!* Birds explode from the branches, shrieking. I stop and watch him. He hugs the tree for a spell, his eyes popping, then, wobbling and wheeling his arms, crashes flat on his back.

The birds make a couple of rounds, settle back in the tree and hush down. With his nose up and his eyes shut, Ivan Ivanych is sprawled out in the flower bed, arms and legs sticking out in all directions. The sole of his shoe has a hole in it, you can see all the way through to his sock. I wait for him to sit up, but he doesn't. From where I stand I can't even tell if he's breathing.

"Ivan Ivanych?" I whisper. "Are you hurt?"

He doesn't stir. This is just plain spooky. A big man like that, not moving, and no one is around to help. Careful not to look into his face, I lean over and press my ear against his chest. Is his heart beating?

His heart beats like a drum.

He snags me into a bear hug, hollering in my ear, "I got you!"

I shove him in the chest and scoot away. What a fool. Why scare me like that? I thought he was dead or something.

He sits up and slaps his hand over his mouth to keep from snorting, that crazy way of laughing. "I'm sorry," he says, though it's plain he's not.

I give him a dirty look. "What did you lie to me for?"

"About what?"

"About being a soccer coach."

"I didn't lie." He shrugs. "Not on purpose. It was a misunderstanding."

"A what?"

"You got the wrong idea and I didn't want to disappoint you." He grins. "To those dads . . . yes . . . I did stretch the truth a little. Their boys were playing soccer on street corners, and all I did was organize them into a team. What's the crime in that? I signed up kids where I thought no one knew us, but that didn't help, did it? You are famous." He snorts again. "But I'm glad it's over. Pretending to be a soccer coach was making me nervous. I feel lighter, you know?" He lifts his face up to the tree branches. "Look at those little fellows," he says. "Not a worry in the world."

The birds skip from branch to branch and because I'm looking, I miss him sneaking out the whistle he used for the drill. When he blows it, I jump. The birds blast out of the tree.

"Go, fellows!" he cries. "Go!"

The birds soar and dive and spiral against the clear sky in one black smudge. It's so beautiful. I forget that I am sore with him. Until the birds are gone and the sky is clear again, then I remember. "What did you do that for?"

"I don't know. For fun?" He offers me the whistle. "Want to try?"

I turn away from him, but when he doesn't say anything for a while, I look back. He sits with his eyes up to the sky, as if turning some important thought in his head.

"I just understood something," he says. "Want me to tell you?"

"No."

"I'll tell you anyway," he says, grinning. "When these grown men chased after their sons around the soccer field, I had a feeling I didn't expect. Envy maybe. I envied them having fun together. Having fun is normal, right? I thought why couldn't Arcady and I have fun? Enjoy a normal life together. Can you understand that?"

"What's there to
understand? I'm not stupid."

"Stupid you're not." He grins and stands
up. "Ready to go?"

I don't move. "You want normal?" I say and look him in the eye. "Going to the tryout is normal. And fun. If those kids are going, why can't I?"

Instead of answering, he begins slapping at his pockets, pulling out scraps of paper with the drills he copied from the soccer manual and shoving them back in until he finds what he's looking for, his hanky. "Don't look at me like that," he says. "You're making me nervous again."

I watch him blow his nose, loud and long.

"Look, Arcady . . . ," he says, and stuffs his hanky back in his pocket. "You heard what that fellow said. We can't go to the tryout without a letter from the school district. It's risky even to ask."

"I'll take the risk," I say.

"You would, wouldn't you?" He shakes his head. "I'll tell you what, Arcady, let me think about it."

I don't say anything. He shakes his head again, grinning now. "Can't you nod your head or say something? Like thank you maybe? Or just smile, Arcady? Come to think of it, I've never even seen you smile. You smile?"

Of course I smile. He just can't see it. I smile mentally, on the inside, not with my mouth.

**NEXT DAY,** he takes me to town. It's the first time since we took that long walk from the children's home to his house a million years ago, but I remember every little thing about it. The red tram and the schoolboys, the smell of freshly baked bread and the cat in the window. But most of all, I remember how happy everyone we passed on the street was for me. I figured everything would be the same today, but it turns out to be different. Instead of smiling at us, people pass by in a hurry. When we cross the street, a bright red tram screeches toward us without slowing down. Ivan Ivanych grabs me by the hand and yanks me off the rails just in time. A policeman standing on the corner blows his whistle and shakes his fist at us. We run.

Soon we come to a crummy building with a big red banner over the door. The words on the banner are too long to spell out. Inside, all kinds of noises come from behind closed doors: people talking, typewriters clacking, radios blasting army marches. Somewhere a telephone rings and rings, and when it stops, someone says, "School district office! What do you want?"

Ivan Ivanych moves from door to door reading what's written on each one.

"Here it is," he says. "Athletic department."

"But we need soccer."

"Don't you know what athletic means? Soccer is included."

"Let's go in then."

"Wait a minute, Arcady," he says. "I think it's a bad idea."

I step around him and knock on the door. He snatches my hand away. "What are you banging like that for?" he whispers. "They're not deaf."

"Come in," a woman's voice sings.

I swing the door open and go in. Ivan Ivanych stays in the doorway.

In the room, smaller even than my bedroom, a woman in a flowery dress clickety-clacks away on a typewriter. She glances at me, smiles, and lifts her pretty eyes to Ivan Ivanych. "Don't tell me. Your boy is ready to be a soccer champion, right?"

"What?" Ivan Ivanych says, startled.

"You need a recommendation letter, don't you?" She plucks a sheet of paper out of her typewriter and holds it up to Ivan Ivanych. "He'll sign it."

"Who?"

"My boss." She nods at yet another door, behind

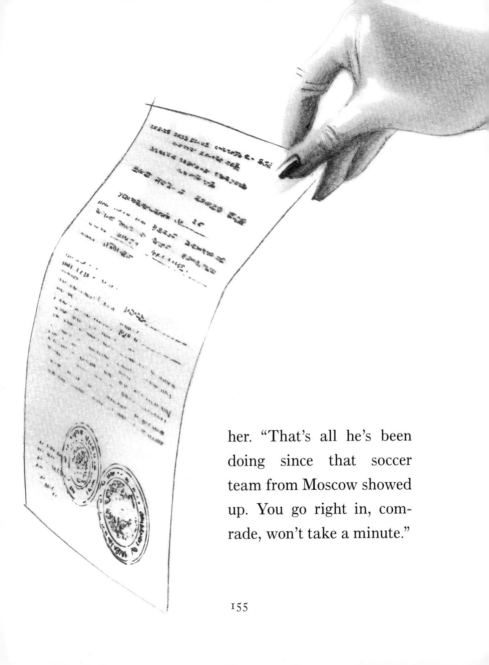

her. "That's all he's been doing since that soccer team from Moscow showed up. You go right in, comrade, won't take a minute."

**I FIGURED** that the boss of athletics would be like Butterball, but he's nothing close. He's a small, skinny guy in a tracksuit and socks, no shoes, sitting on the floor. I can't see his face, only the top of his buzz cut, because he's looking down at a soccer ball jammed between his sharp kneecaps. He's pumping air into the ball, working the hand pump with such fire the ball is about to burst. Somewhere in the room, a radio blaring a marching song makes the windows rattle. Fireball sings along.

Ivan Ivanych knocks on the side of the door, but Fireball doesn't hear over the radio and keeps on pumping. I scan the room. No furniture, no desk, and no chairs, just shelves along the walls loaded with balls, nets, flags, and such. Sporty stuff. But the best things on those shelves are the trophies topped with tiny soccer players. I saw Fedor Brutko holding a trophy like that in the picture in the soccer manual. I wouldn't say no to one of those trophies myself.

Ivan Ivanych knocks a little harder, but Fireball still doesn't hear. I spot the radio box nailed to the wall and move in. Ivan Ivanych tries to stop me, but I'm too quick and pull the plug out. The marching song chokes, but Fireball keeps on singing. When he gets an earful of his hollering without the radio backup, he looks up with a start. *Clonk.* His hand pump drops to the ground.

Fireball stares at Ivan Ivanych. Ivan Ivanych stares at Fireball. Fireball's face turns red, Ivan Ivanych's face, white.

Silence.

Fireball hops up. "Look who's here!" he cries. "Long time no see!"

Ivan Ivanych tries to duck, but Fireball catches him in a hug. I figure Fireball is going to slobber over Ivan Ivanych the way Butterball slobbered over the inspectors, but when Ivan Ivanych glances at me in alarm, Fireball's head swivels in my direction. "This must be Arcady!" He lets go of Ivan Ivanych and rushes at me.

I've got the radio box at my back, so I dart sideways, but he manages to snatch my hand and reel me in. "Heard all about you!" he shouts, pumping my hand as hard as he pumped the soccer ball. "Yes, yes, people are talking."

Fireball drops my hand and runs back to the door. "They take my chairs for meetings and never bring them back," he says to Ivan Ivanych. "How am I supposed to sit down with my friends and have a good chat?" Suddenly, he slaps Ivan Ivanych really hard on the back. "Am I glad to see you, comrade! Won't be a moment," he says and dashes out.

As soon as Fireball is out of sight, Ivan Ivanych is next to me, nudging me toward the door. "We're going."

"Why? What about the letter?"

"Forget about the letter."

He hooks me under the arm and drags me to the door.

"Let me go," I say, and push him away.

At this moment, Fireball is back, hauling in two chairs with their legs out pointing at us like guns. He prods us back into the room. "Sit down, sit down! Make yourselves at home!"

I plop into the chair Fireball slams down. Ivan Ivanych shoots a dirty look at me, missing Fireball's next move. Fireball pushes the second chair under Ivan Ivanych from behind, knocking him off balance. Ivan Ivanych

collapses into the seat. The chair creaks under him.

"One more! One more!" Fireball cries, and bolts out of the room again. Ivan Ivanych follows him with his eyes. "Don't say anything," he says to me. "I'll do all the talking."

Fireball runs back in with another chair and sits down facing us.

"Here we are," he says with a big smile. He looks at Ivan Ivanych as if expecting him to say something, but Ivan Ivanych looks away. Fireball turns to me. Ivan Ivanych said no talking, so I keep my mouth shut.

It's quiet for a while, then Fireball says, "Look at you two, what a picture. The boy, I hear, is a top-notch soccer player, and you, comrade, what now? A soccer coach?" He wags his finger at Ivan Ivanych. "Do we allow such a thing? Coaching children without proper credentials? A violation, comrade, a violation."

Fireball's smile is gone, and his face turns hard. Under his fixed stare, Ivan Ivanych sits still in his wooden chair as if he were made of wood himself.

Fireball bursts out laughing. "Never mind, never mind, just doing my duty. As you see, comrade, I am now a supervisor in charge of the school district's athletics."

Ivan Ivanych squints at Fireball. "You must have done something out of the ordinary to earn such a promotion."

"Not for me to judge," Fireball says, blushing. "Hope to be worthy, that's all."

Ivan Ivanych looks at him long and hard, then shakes his head as if to chase off some thought and says, "Let's just get this over with. We are here to—"

"I'm all ears," Fireball cuts in.

"What we need is—"

"At your service," he cuts in again.

Ivan Ivanych studies him for a second. Fireball beams back. Ivan Ivanych opens his mouth to speak, but Fireball beats him to it. "Mark my words, comrade, your boy has a bright future before him. I hear he scored against the whole team, did he not?" He turns to me. "Scoring goals requires a good head on one's shoulders, Arcady. You must have a good head on your shoulders."

His look confuses me. I can't tell if he's making fun of me or telling me that I'm good.

"I can score with my head," I say just in case.

Fireball slaps his knee and bursts out laughing

again. "Isn't it wonderful? He can score with his head! Do what you want with me, comrade, but I dare say, Arcady is our next Fedor Brutko."

"That's why we are here." Ivan Ivanych holds out the piece of paper that the woman in the flowery dress gave him. "Sign the letter."

Fireball screws his eyes at the piece of paper. "What kind of a letter?"

"You know what kind. To get Arcady into the border guards' camp for a tryout."

"Why me?"

"You are the one signing these letters."

"For you anything, comrade, without hesitation, but . . ." Fireball smiles. "How could I sign it? We don't have any pens here. Look for yourself, no pens, no pencils. We don't write in here, this is athletics."

"Quit clowning. Sign the letter."

"You know how I feel about Arcady. He's our

next Brutko and everything, but . . ." He shrugs. "We don't make the rules, but we must live by them."

"What rules are you talking about?"

"You know what rules. It's easy for you, comrade. Your wife's dead and this boy is no relation of yours. What do you have to lose?"

Ivan Ivanych's left eye twitches. He rubs at it.

"I have family to think about," Fireball goes on. "I'm recently married, my wife's expecting. I can't sign a letter for him."

"Why not?"

"Why not? You must be joking. The boy's parents were enemies of the people!"

Ivan Ivanych stands up quickly and steps toward Fireball. Fireball hops up and darts behind his chair, away from Ivan Ivanych.

"You know what I could do to you?" Ivan Ivanych says. "I could . . ." He clenches his right hand into a fist, crumpling the letter Fireball has refused to sign.

"What is this, comrade? Threatening officials on duty?" Fireball says in a shaky voice. "I can call the law enforcement, it's easy enough. If you didn't learn your lesson yet, they can teach you another. One call from me is all it takes."

At this, Ivan Ivanych staggers back as if hit in the face. The crumpled letter falls from his hand. "Let's go, Arcady," he says without looking at me and storms out of the room.

I'm up and after him, but before I make it to the door, I hear Fireball calling, "Wait, Arcady, wait!"

I turn around and see Fireball plucking a soccer trophy off the shelf and rushing after me. "No hard feelings, Arcady," he says, holding up a trophy. "It's nothing personal, word of honor."

The trophy glows and sparkles in his hands, and at the top, a golden soccer player kicking a golden ball glows and sparkles also. I look over to the door to check with Ivan Ivanych, but he's nowhere in sight. Instead, that pretty woman in the flowery dress is looking into the room, nodding and smiling. "Take it, dear," she says. "Take it."

I turn back to Fireball, grab the trophy, and run out.

**IVAN IVANYCH** is marching way up ahead of me and he won't slow down. I'm rushing after him with the trophy under my arm. Before I know it, we are in a part of town I've never been to before. Crooked

buildings lean into one another as if unsteady on their feet. Rude pictures are scribbled on fences. Heavy trucks thunder by.

Ivan Ivanych turns toward a screwy old building black from age or soot with a sign stuck over the door. T . . . E . . . A . . . I spell the word on the sign, as we climb the creaky steps. R . . . O . . . O . . . M. Tearoom.

When he swings the door open, I get a peek of what's inside. It's a dump. Dark and smoky and smelling of something sour, the room is packed with loud men, each face redder than the next.

"What are we doing here?" I say.

"I'm thirsty," he growls and dives in. The door snaps shut behind him.

I stare at the door for a moment, then run down the stairs, plant my rear on the bottom step and look at my soccer trophy. I'm sort of confused. Why did I get the trophy but not the letter? What happened? Ivan Ivanych and Fireball knew each other from before. There was something bad between them, but what? Usually I know what's going on, but now I'm not coming up with anything. I set the trophy next to me on the step and look around.

The tearoom is squeezed in between other grimy buildings along the dirt road. Smack in the middle of the road, a bunch of birds are pecking in the dust. Heavy trucks rumble back and forth roaring like cannon fire. The whole street shudders, but the birds don't care. They wait until the giant tires just about squash them then burst in all directions. The trucks thunder by and, before the dust settles, the stubborn birds are back. I like the birds, they never quit.

Then one of the trucks angles off the road. Piling up dust, it grinds to a halt in front of the tearoom. The driver gets out, banging the door shut. He hustles to the rear of the truck and slides the bolts off the tailboard. As the tailboard swivels over with a bang, I recognize him. The driver is Redhead, who told Ivan Ivanych about the tryout. I watch him pull one box out of the truck bed, then another and then a third. Each box is full of bottles. He stacks them up and hauls them toward the steps where I am sitting.

"Arcady? What are you doing here alone?"

"Waiting."

"For Ivan Ivanych? Where is he?"

"In there."

He glances up at the door to the tearoom and wags his head as if he thinks it's a bad idea for Ivan Ivanych to be there. Then he goes up the steps with his boxes full of clinking bottles, pushes at the door with his rear, and before the door snaps shut after him, he shouts toward his truck, "Grishka! Look who's here!"

A small red head pops over the sideboard. It's Freckles. When he sees me, he leaps over the sideboard and runs up to me so fast our knees knock. He springs back, blushes, and begins talking, fidgeting the whole time.

"Isn't it great? Isn't it just? I was so hoping to see you again but nobody knows where you live. I asked everyone. It's a secret, right? A secret? You don't have to tell me if you don't want to. It's all right."

He giggles and keeps going *tra-ta-ta,* like a machine gun.

"What are you doing here? Waiting for someone? Your pals, right? You have lots of pals? Do you want to know something? Why my dad put me on the soccer team? Not because of soccer. He wanted me to make friends! Isn't that funny?"

He fake laughs and blushes again.

"We had another practice today. Boring! Not the same without you. Where's number ten, right?

That's what our coach said, Where's number ten?
Did you know they found a new coach already? He
used to be a real soccer player. But so what, right?
He never even listens when you ask him something.
I liked Ivan Ivanych more. Was that place where he
got you from really bad? The children's home, I
mean. You don't mind me asking? It wasn't bad,
right? All your pals and no parents? Nobody telling
you what to do? Just play and play! Do you want to
play sometimes? With me, I mean. It's all right if
you don't want to. Because you only play soccer,
right? Quick, quick, quick, that's you!"

He jerks this way and that, pretending to be on
the ball. It looks all wrong but I keep quiet watching. He kicks the pretend ball and throws his arms
up as if he's scored a goal.

"Go-o-o-o-al!" he shouts and beams a huge smile
at me. "When will you go to Rakitino for the tryout?
All the boys on the team got their letters to go. If
you pass the tryout, they'll take you to Moscow with

them for good. Did you know that? Not that I would ever get on the team, but if I did, I wouldn't go. Moscow is far away. I'd miss my dad."

He rolls his eyes, thinking of what else he wants to tell me. Then his whole face lights up like a lightbulb.

"Do you want to try out together? Wouldn't that be fun? My dad could take us in his truck. He and Ivan Ivanych could ride in the cabin and you and I in the back. I always ride in the back with the boxes. It's fun! Do you want to?"

I look at his huge eyes, his red hair sticking out every which way, his crazy freckles, and when I shake my head no, he winces as if I slapped him.

Then he just stands there, not knowing what to do, and since he stopped talking, he spots my soccer trophy. His eyes grow bigger than before.

"Whoa," he says. "Look at that! A real soccer trophy. Where did you get it?"

I shrug.

"They only give these to the soccer champions! Are you on a champion team now? You won this?"

"I didn't win it. Someone gave it to me."

"Who?"

"The guy in charge of signing letters for the tryout."

"He did? But why? Why did he give it to you?"

"I don't know. I wish he'd sign my letter instead."

"He didn't sign it?" He stares at me in alarm. "But then—"

The tearoom door flies open and Redhead stomps down the steps. Freckles throws himself in his path. "Dad! Dad! Wait! Arcady can't go to the tryout! That man who signed our letter, remember? He didn't sign Arcady's letter!"

Redhead glances at me and nudges Freckles toward the truck.

"Nothing we can do about it, son. Get in."

"But Dad?"

"Get in, I said."

He slams the tailboard and wants to bolt it, but Freckles hangs onto his arm. His dad gives him a rough shove, bolts in the tailboard, and when he turns around, Freckles's eyes are filling up with water. His dad gasps, rushes up to Freckles and gathers him into a hug. Freckles starts weeping.

"Don't cry, Grishutka," Redhead says, biting his lip so as not to cry himself. "Forgive this old fool. I didn't mean to—"

The tearoom door flies open again and Ivan Ivanych steps out. He grabs at the railing and plants his legs wide apart as if he's on a boat in the storm. He looks at Redhead hugging his son. "Weeping?" he says, smacking his lips. "Do we allow such a thing?"

He catches me staring at his face, which is as red as those other men's faces in the tearoom. He grins stupidly. I turn away.

Redhead wipes his son's wet cheeks with his coat sleeve, whispering softly into his ear. Freckles looks at him, smiles a tiny smile and climbs into the cabin of the truck. In a moment, he's out again, clutching something in his hand. He heads back to me, not as fast this time. "Dad had to write my name on it, but it's in pencil," he says, sniffling. "You can erase it and fill in yours. Easy."

I look at a piece of paper he's holding out to me. It is his recommendation letter. I crane my neck over at Ivan Ivanych. He frowns, lets go of the railing as if to step down, lurches sideways and grabs the railing again.

"Take it, Arcady," Freckles says. "They won't let you in without the letter."

"But what about you?"

"I don't really want to go to the tryout. I won't pass it anyhow. I just want to go with you for a ride in the truck."

"For definite?"

He nods. "Yes, yes. Take it."

I shrug.

"Thanks, pal." I take the letter and, in turn, hand him the soccer trophy. "You take this then."

Freckles's mouth drops open and his eyes turn as big as the wheels on his dad's truck. He holds up the trophy for his dad to see. Redhead smiles at his kid, and looks up at Ivan Ivanych at the top of the stairs.

"Rakitino is far away, Ivan Ivanych," he says. "If you fill her up, you're welcome to borrow my truck. She's not much of a vehicle, but she'll get you there and back."

"Much obliged, comrade," Ivan Ivanych says. "But we won't be needing it."

He lifts his chin up, proud-like, strides off the porch, and, missing a step, tumbles down the stairs.

**I SLICE UP BREAD,** two slices each, and fill the bowls with the soup we made together. The soup is red because of the beets. The color makes me think of the picture of Fedor Brutko on the cover of the soccer manual. I wonder if he'll be in his red gear when I show up. Because thanks to the letter Freckles gave me, Ivan Ivanych has no choice but to take me to the tryout.

From now on, Freckles is my pal. He wanted to show me what fun it is to ride in the truck bed. I pretended it was my first time, keeping hushed about those other times I rode in the truck bed when the guards hauled me from one dump to another. But with Freckles it was fun. Every time we went over a rut or a pothole, he'd fake flying out of the truck bed, laughing like crazy.

Ivan Ivanych didn't want to ride with us, but his legs were too wobbly to walk. He sat in the cabin with Freckles's dad. It was no tea Ivan Ivanych was drinking in the tearoom, of course, I wasn't born yesterday. I've seen the guards at the children's home drunk night after night.

I wait for Ivan Ivanych at the table with a piece of cloth on my knees, a napkin. He likes for me to keep it in my lap while we eat. Except we're not eating. After Redhead dropped us off, Ivan Ivanych went into his room and hasn't come out. I've been sitting for ages listening to my belly rumble.

There's so much about Ivan Ivanych I can't figure out. First off, his soccer team. Why go to the trouble of taking me in if he's not a soccer coach? Of course, I knew he wasn't a coach. Maybe my head didn't, but my gut knew for definite. Didn't I watch him copying things from the soccer manual at night? Scribbling away on tiny scraps of paper? Hiding the scraps in different pockets before the first drill? And did he ever touch the ball? Not once. Plain as day he knew zero about soccer. And another thing. That Fireball. He knew Ivan Ivanych's wife had died. Something feels really bad about that, but what?

**I PRESS MY EAR** against his door, listening. Not
a peep. I knock, but he doesn't answer. I crack the
door open and peek into his room, no bigger than
mine. He's slouched in a chair by the window, looking out.

"The soup is getting cold."

He starts and turns slowly as if waking from a
dream. "Ah, it's you, Arcady."

"Who else would it be?"

We eyeball each other.

"What are you doing?" I say.

"Me?" His chair creaks as he shifts a little. "I'm talking to someone."

No one else is in there, just him. "Talking to who?"

"My wife," he says. "Natasha." He nods at a picture in a frame sitting on the windowsill, just a dark shape against the window light. I step in to take a look. A girl is in the picture, smiling.

"How come she's so young?"

## CHAPTER TWENTY-NINE

"She was young," he says. "Just turned twenty-two when they took her away."

"Who took her away?"

He studies me for a spell, considering. "Shut the window," he says so softly it is almost a whisper.

It's not cold in his room, but I do what he says. I shut the window and perch myself on the window-sill next to the picture. "Who took her away?"

"The police. They took her right out of her class-room. Natasha taught German in our school. I taught Russian there, that was how we met. Another teacher accused her of being a German spy. She was no spy, of course, but the police believed him. They always do."

A ray of sun cuts through the window and catches a glint in his eye. He blinks and turns his face from me.

"What happened to your wife after they took her away?"

"Same as what happens to others they call enemies of the people. Same as what happened to your parents, Arcady."

I look at the picture. His wife is smiling at me, but when I move forward just a bit to see her face better, light from the window floods the picture-frame glass and her face melts away.

"You never saw her again?"

"I tried to visit her in prison, but they wouldn't let me. I insisted so they took me in, too. To teach me a lesson, they said."

"Then what?"

He doesn't answer, just sits there, hushed, staring at nothing.

"Then what?"

He glances at me then at the picture, leans in and lays the picture facedown as though he doesn't want his wife to hear what he's saying.

"The police are good at teaching lessons, Arcady. Afterward, the one in charge told me it was best to forget Natasha. Take my advice, he said, don't stick your neck out. From now on, take no risks."

"What did you do?"

"Took his advice. After I got back here, I locked myself in. For a long time I didn't leave this house."

"How long?"

"I don't remember. Weeks."

"But what did you eat?"

"Strawberry jam left over from Natasha. She made plenty."

"You lived on strawberry jam? Not bad."

He smiles. "Since then can't eat it. What's left is yours."

"So you are not a soccer coach and you are not an inspector either? You are a schoolteacher?"

"Used to be, but I never went back to our school. I decided to look for work where no one knew me. When a place turned up with the children's home inspection, I put a false name down and wrote 'never been married' on my application. They didn't check. No matter what I saw in those children's homes, I kept my mouth shut. I took no risks. Until I saw you, that is. That soccer of yours was rough, but you stood up to the bigger guys. You took such risks, I felt ashamed. Oh, so ashamed, Arcady. You inspired me to go up against your director. What was that you called him?"

## CHAPTER TWENTY-NINE

"Butterball?"

"Yes. Butterball." He smiles. "It felt good to scold Butterball, really good. I was surprised I still had that much feeling left in me. Do you understand, Arcady? You woke me up."

**WE SIT AT THE TABLE.** My soup is long gone, but he's yet to touch his.

"You don't like it?" I say.

"What?"

"The soup."

He looks at his bowl as if surprised to find it there and picks up his spoon. I watch him stir his soup without eating.

"Why did that teacher do it?"

"What teacher?"

"The one who lied to the police about your wife."

"Oh, him? Who knows? He got a promotion."

"For lying?"

Ivan Ivanych shrugs. "He used to be a physical education instructor, but now he's in charge of the school district's athletics. You met him today. He refused to sign your letter, Arcady."

The room gets terribly quiet. So quiet I can't stand it. I want to jump up, stomp my boots, kick something, promise him that I will kill Fireball. But I know it's stupid. I won't kill anyone, so instead I stay in my seat and say, "Why did the police believe such scum?"

"Arcady! Don't talk like that."

"I want to know. Why do they arrest people for nothing? None of my pals in the children's home knew. I asked everyone."

Ivan Ivanych looks at his spoon, blinks, and gently sets it back down.

"Some say it's because the war is coming," he

says. "The government figures that if they take away our loved ones, we'll have nothing to lose. That would make us fight better. But I don't know the real reason, Arcady. Nobody really does."

He picks up his spoon and starts eating. I watch him for a while, thinking. The government figured

it all wrong. Everyone knows it's easy to fight when you have nothing to lose, but you fight harder when you have something to keep. Most likely Ivan Ivanych was never much of a fighter, but taking his wife away didn't make him into a better one. I was always good at fighting, but now I have to be better, twice as good to fight for both of us.

Just as I think that—*bang!*—Something strikes the windowpane.

Ivan Ivanych's spoon clinks into the bowl, splashing the tablecloth with red splotches. "What was that?" he cries.

I run out.

**IT'S SO SLIGHT**, just a handful of fluff. Stiff twiggy legs, soft yellow belly. The beak is open a little, but the eyes are shut. I cup my hands together to keep the breeze from snatching it. Ivan Ivanych bends over me to look. "Poor thing," he says. "Want to bury him?"

"Why? He's not dead."

I close my palms and shake it gently. Wake up, bird.

"He's dead, Arcady. Nobody lives through a knock that hard."

I give the bird a good shake.

"Stop, Arcady."

I shake it again, faster.

"What are you doing?"

I walk away from him, shaking my cupped hands wildly.

"Arcady!" he shouts and charges after me. I wheel away, but he lunges at my hands, catches me by the wrist, and begins to pry my hands open.

"Leave me alone!" I yell and swing my hands away, aiming to nail him with my elbow. We struggle, but Ivan Ivanych is stronger. He brings me down and pulls my hands apart.

*Zoom!*

With a cheep, the bird flies out, brushing my fingers with its beating wings.

"Whoa!" I cry. "Did you see that?"

The bird zigzags through the trees and plunges into the leaves high above, kicking off a riot of chirping.

"I told you he was alive."

## CHAPTER THIRTY-ONE

Ivan Ivanych steps away from me, trying not to look embarrassed. "You were right," he says. "Good job." And he walks up the steps to the house.

"When are we going to the tryout?"

He half turns to me in the doorway. "What?"

"When are we going to the tryout? I got us the letter."

Ivan Ivanych shakes his head and steps into the house.

**WE KEEP A TIN PAIL** by the door for things we throw away, potato peels, burned-out matches, rags and such. When I follow him into the house, I see he's thrown his soccer manual in there. I pull it out. "What did you do that for?"

He pays me no mind, and marches toward his room. I cut him off at the door. "You're related to an enemy of the people same as I am, right?"

"Keep your voice down. I should never have told you."

"Take me to the tryout, and I'll clear our names for good, I promise."

He rolls his eyes and wants to open the door, but I block it. "You saw me score a goal. I'm a great scorer."

"Move aside."

"If I score a goal for the Red Army, you know what will happen? I will become a soccer champion!"

"I am asking you nicely. Please move aside."

"You could be my coach if you want. I won't tell a soul you're not really a coach, I promise. The two of us could be champions."

"Move aside!"

"Listen to me, this is important! If we are champions who'd dare to treat us like enemies? Nobody. We could be like everybody else, like regular people!"

He raises his hand to grab me, but I duck and step aside. He glares at me and grips the doorknob. "Don't you understand what happened today in the school district's office? One call from that man, and they will arrest me and send you back to the children's home. We won't see each other ever again! We are in danger, and you decide to become like everybody else by standing out! Why can't you just do what regular boys do, Arcady?"

"Like what?"

"I don't know. Go climb a tree."

He yanks the door open. His hand flies back, but the door stays put. He looks at the doorknob in his hand then at the round hole in the door. He shoots me a sore look, shoves the doorknob back

into the hole and twists it in. When he moves his hand away, the doorknob drops to the floor next to his shoe. I never heard him cuss before, but he's doing it now and kicking the doorknob hard. It rolls in a loop and bumps against his shoe again.

"Pass," I say.

He lifts his eyes at me. "What?"

"Pass the ball."

It takes him a spell to get my meaning. But he's not stupid, he figures it out. He grins and kicks the knob toward me. His kick is lousy, but I step in to cut the knob on the go and kick it back to him. He scrapes his shoes together, heel to heel, to trap the knob. I dart across the room. "Over here! Pass!" He kicks the knob my way, but it loops into the wall. I get it on the rebound.

"Pass!" he yells.

We kick the doorknob back and forth, spinning it between the walls and under the table and through chair legs. Then I kick the knob a little too hard and it smacks him in the shin.

"Ouch," he cries, clutching at his leg. "What the hell, Arcady!" He hops one-legged to the table and leans on it, panting.

"Sorry," I say. "Does it hurt?"

He flings himself into the chair. "Not a bit."

"Are you scared to take me to the tryout?"

"Scared?" He fake snorts. "Of course not!" He snatches the spoon and begins shoveling soup fast into his mouth, slurping. I'm watching him. He flashes his eyes at me, leans back, and whacks the spoon against the table. "Why do you always have to stick your neck out?"

"You stuck your neck out on me."

"But it was worth it, can't you see? This is a second chance for both of us. Why tempt fate?"

"You know what?" I squint at him to make sure. "You *are* scared."

**WHEN I WAKE UP,** the house is quiet. He's not in the front room, so I knock on his door, but he doesn't answer. I lean toward the circle of light where the doorknob used to be and peek in. The room is empty. He always warns me if he has to go someplace, but last night after I said he was scared, he stopped talking.

Still he left breakfast for me on the table. In a patch of sunlight, a plate is waiting with a slice of bread spread with strawberry jam and a glass of milk. The strawberry jam glistens and, turning thickly over the edges, slides down the sides of the bread, making puddles. I look but I can't eat it, not after he told me he lived on this strawberry jam when he was too spooked to go out.

I take the plate to the open window, scrape the jam off the bread with a knife, break the bread into the smallest pieces, and set the plate on the windowsill. I don't have to wait long for the birds to come nosing around. In no time, the bread is gone, crumbs included. I wash the plate, suit up in my soccer gear, and go out.

Hanging on a rope tied between two trees is a tablecloth, rippling a little in the breeze. Last night Ivan Ivanych was sore at me but he took it out on the tablecloth. He scrubbed and scrubbed the thing, but the soup he splashed on it when the bird hit the window is still there, as red as before.

I knee the ball over the tablecloth, dive under the rope, trap the ball with my chest and kick it back over. I do that a few times, but it gets boring. I run the ball in loops around the house and beat a couple of trees on the dribble. The trees just stand there. I'd rather be knocking the doorknob with Ivan Ivanych than this. The trouble with soccer, you can't play it alone.

After I broke that window with my spinner, Ivan Ivanych outlawed using the house as a backstop. He turned down my idea of fixing up the broken window with boards and instead hauled in a fresh piece of glass from someplace. We nearly cracked the glass while setting it into the frame, and yesterday that bird just about took it out again. The last thing I want is to crack the glass and make him sore again, but before I know it, I'm in the back of the house making the most of his wall.

*Thud.*

*Thud.*

*Thud.*

I whip the wall switching feet. Left and right. Right and left. When the ball bounces back, I kick it again. No spinning. Straight on the nose and not too hard. Target practice. Shoot for the corners. Top and bottom. Dead center.

Ivan Ivanych's house is made of logs, and my last ball knocks one of the logs out of joint. The ball bounces back, but not low enough to give it a boot. A diving header height. I line myself with the ball, knees bent, hands out to break the fall. The timing is important. When the ball comes, I dive in headfirst.

Then a strange thing happens. The logs in the wall wobble and fade away, and instead of the back

wall, I see a soccer goal with a goalie. I fly toward the goal and at the same time see myself flying—in the Red Army red, number ten.

"Mark ten! Mark ten!" the goalie growls, spreading his gloved hands post to post. Giant defenders spring out of nowhere, turning the air so thick with their sweat you could use it for a rebound. They leap up to block the goal, leaving only a tight opening in the far corner. I drive into the ball. *Smack!* Anyone would blink on impact, but I keep my eyes open. I want to see the ball going in. In it goes.

Go-o-o-o-o-o-al!

The Red Army fans climb over the fences and run across the turf to hug me. The guards with barking dogs from the children's home turn up to cut them off, but nothing can stop the fans, they roll over the guards like a steamroller.

"Hooooray!"

My teammates lift me up into their arms. "He's a natural!" they holler. "Born for soccer!"

Fedor Brutko's face floats up. "You are a soccer champion now, Arcady," he shouts over the roar. "Welcome to my team!"

Then all at once it's not the fans cheering, but the birds screeching. Fedor Brutko melts away, and my teammates and the fans also. The house wall is back as it was before, one log is out of joint. Up above, the birds zoom in and out of the slanted sunbeams in panic. My header scared them. Worse, I headed the ball all the way up the same tree the yellow-bellied bird flew into after I shook it to life. My ball is lodged into the crook of a branch, as high as the sky.

**I'VE NEVER DONE** this before. Climbing, I mean. It was against the rules in the children's home. But climbing is a piece of cake. My muscles are strong and I'm quick. In no time, I am halfway up the tree.

It's a high tree with branches sticking out every which way. At the bottom, just twigs, most broken off, but at the top, a mess of branches full of leaves and birds. It is the greatest thing to climb a tree, I never knew. You stretch your hand up, get a grip, push off with the other elbow or else a knee. Up and up and up. I grab on tight and feel where to put my feet, testing the branches first. Can they hold me?

## CHAPTER THIRTY-FOUR

Then one hand on, one off, climbing and breathing in deep.

My face is close to the wrinkled bark, almost touching, I can't see what's around. If I look down, a funny feeling swells up from the soles of my boots to my belly. To look up, I have to lean with my shoulders away from the tree and straighten my arms, but this is a little scary. What if a branch comes off in your hand? What would happen? You'd just get killed, smash your head open. There's nothing to see above anyhow, just sky.

It's hard to tell how high I've come until I'm right underneath my ball that's stuck in the crook of the branch. I know it's high without looking. I feel the tree moving because of the wind. The ball is off to the right and one branch up. I stretch my hand for it, fingertips reaching but not touching. Just a little bit more. A little bit more. Straining, I push off with my toes from the branch below and leap, trying to knock the ball to the ground. For one tiny second I'm not holding on to the tree. My heart skips, thump-a-thump. My chest quivers. I am in the air. I'm weightless. I'm a bird.

My hand misses the ball but grips the branch below, and when the branch bends too quickly, I know it will not hold. It snaps off in a burst of brown splinters, and I drop straight down, crashing through the branches and leaves. It's a noisy fall, and it hurts, but halfway down, I grab at something that breaks the fall.

Hanging from a branch and panting, I'm trying

to get my breath back when my ball swooshes past, falling through the leaves. It takes a long time for the ball to hit the ground below. I listen to the far-off sound of the ball bouncing and, when it stops, I begin swinging back and forth, faster and faster, kicking my feet through the air, to pull myself up to the top of the branch, but this doesn't work. I stop kicking and just hang, resting.

I force myself to look down. First I see that my soccer shirt is ripped, my right knee is bleeding and one boot is gone. Down below, a thick carpet of leaves covers the roof of our house from before I moved in. My ball is a dot in the grass. My arms are sore, and so are my chest and shoulders, but I hang tight. I won't let go until Ivan Ivanych gets home.

**I'M LOSING STRENGTH** and what's left of my hope when a sound comes, a motor engine of some kind, a vehicle. I hear it pulling up, brakes screeching. The engine coughs and chokes, a door creaks open then shuts with a bang. In a moment, Ivan Ivanych, whistling and swinging his briefcase, enters the orchard. By the funny way he is walking, almost skipping, I can tell he is happy about something. The ball in the grass stops him. He quits whistling, stares at the ball for a moment then looks around. Not finding me, he picks up the ball, drops it on his foot and tries juggling. He is no better with the ball than he was with the doorknob. I can't see him going into the house, but I know he did because I hear him calling for me inside, probably poking his head into my room, then into his, opening the door to the bathroom and getting worried.

"Arcady!"

Now he's outside again, circling the house, looking. He stops near the hanging tablecloth. "Arcady! Where are you?"

I want to shout, "I'm here, look up in the tree," but my throat is so thick I can't make a peep. And it's just awful, just horrible, listening to him calling my name and not being able to answer. It's the worst ever. If he weren't so soft, so easily scared, I would call to him somehow. But I know what will happen if he sees me up in this tree. He'll lose it. He might even start crying.

"Arcady! Arcady! Come back, please!"

I begin shaking like it's cold and my fingers dig deeper into the bark, but I'm barely holding on. All this shaking makes the branch go *crack* and drop a bit lower, jolting me.

Ivan Ivanych looks up. "Arcady!" he wails. He takes off running, doesn't watch where he's going, and runs smack into the tablecloth. The rope snaps off at both ends, and he tumbles through the grass wrapped up in cloth, trying to kick himself free and growling like a wild animal.

A second jolt, then—*snap!*—*whoosh!*—I'm falling. Air blasts through my shorts, leaves and branches flicker by, whipping me in the face, and just as I am about to hit the ground, Ivan Ivanych catches me in his arms wrapped in tablecloth.

"I got you!"

I never let anyone in my life see me cry, not ever, but this time I lose it. He draws me in to his chest, hugging me so deeply I feel his heart beating wildly against my cheek.

**KA-BOOM!**

"Hear that thunder?" Ivan Ivanych shouts over the rattle of the truck. "A storm's on the way!"

Out the window there's nothing to look at: just corn, a dirt road up ahead, and clouds of dust. We bounce up and down in our seat. I'm the passenger and Ivan Ivanych is the driver, the two of us in the cabin. Redhead kept his promise and gave us his truck. Now Ivan Ivanych is taking it extra slow. Turtle speed. I have my doubts he ever drove a truck before.

"Mind if I ask you something?" I say.

"Ask away."

"Why did you change your mind?"

"About what?"

"About taking me to the tryout. Not scared anymore?"

He scowls at me. The moment he takes his eyes off the road, the truck swerves, and we're heading straight for the ditch.

"Look out!"

He panics and spins the steering wheel one way, then the other, but after a spell puts us back on course. "Who said I was scared?" he says.

"I did."

He snorts and shakes his head. "I guess being around a risk taker like you, Arcady, some of it had to rub off on me."

*Ka-boom!* Thunder again.

He glances at the black clouds shaping up ahead and does something to the truck to make it lurch forward. The soccer ball in my lap bounces to the floor.

"We'll beat this storm, Arcady, don't you worry."

"I'm not worried."

"Do you ever?"

The truck flies over ruts and potholes. My soccer ball dances under the dashboard.

"You know I'll pass the tryout," I say.

"*I know* you'll do your best."

"I'll pass it. But if the Red Army takes me on, will I have to go to Moscow with them?"

"You might."

"What about you? Will I have to leave you behind?"

He glances at me. The truck swerves, but he controls it nicely. "I'm glad you asked," he says. "I hear they have a big problem in Moscow. Plenty of soccer coaches, not enough schoolteachers. A real shortage, I hear. I'm hoping that after you become a soccer champion, they'll let me go back to teaching." He snorts. "Boys like you don't fall off of trees very often. I'd better pack up and go with you. What do you think, Arcady? Would that be all right?"

I stare at him. He made up that big problem in Moscow, but I don't care. He said what I wanted to hear.

The truck bounces over a bump in the road and my soccer ball leaps back into my lap.

"You said you put a fake name on the application to join the inspectors," I say.

"I had to."

"Your name is not Ivan Ivanych then?"

"No, it's not."

"It's not Coach, either," I say. "So what should I call you?"

"Try Dad."

I smile at him. Not mentally on the inside like before. I smile at him with my mouth. In real life.

# AUTHOR'S NOTE

In the summer of 2013, at Oakland University in Michigan, I delivered a lecture on the psychological and emotional effects of Stalinism. The students seemed shocked by the fact that despite terrible crimes committed against the Russian people by their own government, no one ever spoke out openly against the government or sought justice, and those few who dared to speak did so privately and in a whisper.

After I finished the lecture, a car came to take me to the airport. The driver flung my bag into the trunk, slammed it shut, and bellowed with a thick Russian accent, "Hello! I am Yury from St. Petersburg!" It is not often that I encounter someone from my hometown, so the whole way to the airport we chatted pleasantly in Russian until Yury learned the reason for my visit to Michigan. He fell silent. I watched his face in the rear-view mirror. He was clearly struggling with some troubling thought. At last, his eyes met mine in the mirror and he said, "Stalin sent my grandfather to the hard labor camp for ten years. After they let him out, he died. He was too weak to go on." I caught myself leaning in close to hear Yury. He was *whispering*.

And so it goes. The terror inflicted upon the Russian people by Stalinism did not die with those who experienced it firsthand but continued on from one generation to the next. It is as if anyone born in the Soviet Union continued to suffer from a post-traumatic stress disorder that has never been treated. The reason for this is simple. With the very formation of the Soviet Union, millions of innocent people were arrested, exiled, or executed as enemies of the people. Anxious about *potential* opposition, the Communist Party that ruled the Soviet Union destroyed anyone who *might* disagree with its regime. The terror associated with such *preemptive* strikes traumatized Russian people for years to come. The Communist Party ensured that this trauma would live on even after the demise of Communism. It did so by shattering the families of the enemies of the people. Their family members were denied places to live, work permits, and food rations. Children suffered the most. Infants were separated from their mothers, placed into the security-police-run orphanages, and often given different surnames. The older children, termed "socially dangerous elements," were tried under adult criminal laws; the death penalty was meted out to twelve-year-olds. Everything was taken away from these children: homes, parents, siblings, identities, health, and too often their very lives. Small wonder that the children of the enemies of the people dreamed of overcoming their stigma and becoming like everybody else, regular people. They wanted to live normal lives free of shame and discrimination. Some sought opportunities to redeem their stigma, while others went on to lead double lives in an attempt to keep their identities secret. None would speak openly about their parents' fate.

And that is why sixty years after the death of Stalin and thousands of miles away from Russia, Yury from St. Petersburg, who drove me to the Detroit airport, fell to whispering as he shared the fate of his grandfather, an enemy of the people. At that moment my heart ached for Yury. My heart ached for myself also. My heart ached for all of us born in the Soviet Union and traumatized by Stalinism. A line of poetry rang out in my mind from Osip Mandelstam, a Russian poet who on Stalin's personal order perished in a concentration camp: "I could have whistled through life starling-like, nibbling on nut pies, but it seems off limits for me."

*—Eugene Yelchin*
*Los Angeles, September 2013*